# The Last Christmas Card

Laura Briggs

This is a work of fiction. Names, places, characters, and events are a product of the author's imagination. Any resemblance between characters and persons either living or dead is purely coincidental.

**The Last Christmas Card**

COPYRIGHT © 2014 by Laura Briggs

ISBN-13: 978-1502824233

ISBN-10: 150282423X

All rights reserved. No part of this book maybe used or reproduced without the author's permission.

Cover: "Christmas Past." Original photograph, "Old ornament and vintage Christmas Card" courtesy Aliced at Dreamstime.com.

To the men and women of the military
in thanks for all their sacrifices.

And

To my grandfathers who served
in times of war and uncertainty.

*The Last Christmas Card*

Samantha Sowerman turned the key in the lock and pushed open the door. It resisted, the wood sticking to the painted frame and parting with a sigh as it whooshed open with a blast of cool air. The smell of stale rooms and dust from the empty foyer.

The Boston brownstone was only half-renovated; that was the reason rent was cheap for a post-college vagabond in search of a temporary home. Perfect for Samantha, who never parked her bags anywhere for long. Not since her mother's late-stage cancer diagnosis meant the end of home.

She sneezed as she carried her knapsack and duffel bag through the main hall, a film of dust coating her kinky blond hair. Green wallpaper decorated with roses trailed in strips from the walls in the main hall. Thick dust like a carpet over the dark walnut floors, fading an area rug left carelessly at the foot of the stairs.

*The Last Christmas Card*

Her apartment was the one on the main floor—the only one with running water at the moment, apparently. The owner Mrs. Lindell had inherited the house from a more wealthy relative and planned to transform the three stories into a series of spacious apartments to attract tenants with an interest in living in one of the historic neighborhoods. Samantha's space had once been the downstairs parlor and dining room, now a bedroom and sitting area with two spaces walled off for the kitchen and bathroom. A narrow shower and repurposed cabinets stripped here and there of retro orange paint.

Above the doorway to the bedroom was an old-fashioned framed sampler: *For what you give us, Lord, make us truly thankful.*

"Somebody must have been a spiritual brother or sister," she said, touching the dusty frame with one hand. Her fingers just barely reached it.

*The Last Christmas Card*

    These days she had nobody to talk to but God, and the occasional distant relative who sent her a card or a letter to make sure everything was all right. But Samantha was used to being on her own; used to being a constant movement in the world. Like a seed bursting from a dandelion head, waiting a push from the wind.

    After college, it was a mission trip to Botswana. An agricultural outreach ministry in Australia. Two months spent on the inner city streets of New York working at a homeless shelter–and now, half a year as the editor of a church outreach journal.

    "We're not looking for anybody permanent, Miss Sowerman. Just someone to write a series on mission travel. If you're interested, we'd love to publish your pieces for this year's journals." The publisher's email from *Global Outreach* had reached her inbox less than a month after she returned from a brief mission assignment in Puerto Rico.

It was the perfect break for her; the chance to rest between experiences and earn a little to apply to her college loans. All she needed was a place to live, anywhere she could find a space that would let her camp for six months to a year.

That's when she found an online ad for the brownstone apartment under renovation.

"You won't have any neighbors," Mrs. Lindell informed her over the phone. "The rest of the building is pretty much under construction right now. You know, building a bathroom in the basement, putting a kitchen upstairs, etc."

"That's fine," Samantha answered. "I mean, I'm not afraid to be alone in the building if that's what you're thinking."

"The noise level will be a little loud for awhile," said her future landlady. "But most of it will

*The Last Christmas Card*

be in the basement. If you need a place to store some stuff, I can let you use a room upstairs until they're ready to start that apartment."

Samantha laughed. "I travel light, so the extra space isn't necessary," she answered. "I think the apartment's size will be perfect for me."

And it was. A few posters of Africa on the wall, a framed honeymoon photo of her parents and a few of her friends from college. The group photo from her missionary stint in Australia propped on the dresser next to an antique basin left in the room and her battered Bible. In the closet, she found a locked tin box, now piled with her spare sneakers splattered with paint and tie-dyed t-shirts with church camp slogans.

She tacked up the poster of her next great adventure on the wall and stepped back to smile at the scene of two village children playing against a vivid sunset. One of her friends from Botswana had told her

*The Last Christmas Card*

about it, a mission experience as an interpreter for a farm and medical mission in South America. Her Spanish was good, made better with practice in Puerto Rico. There was an opening in the spring; all she had to do was pay her way to the village in Brazil.

With a sigh, she sank down on the bed, leaning back with eyes closed. An old quilt was draped across its end, stitched with blackbirds and red sunflowers. It reminded her of one when she was a little girl. Her mother tied the corners with bright yarn in red and yellow.

Even though her own quilt had fallen to pieces years ago, it was still alive in her memory as she snuggled beneath the musty folds later that night.

*****

*The Last Christmas Card*

Silence echoed in the hallways of the house, drifting from doors ajar upstairs and half-finished rooms. Samantha had walked through them out of curiosity, interested to see the rest of her temporary home. Stained glass windows filtered light in rose and yellow on the second floor, skeleton walls visible in the future apartment and the old bathroom, where a claw foot tub resided with rows of narrow copper pipes half-torn from the wall.

At the top of the stairs was a narrow passage that opened to the attic. She turned the rattling knob and peered inside. Shawls of cobweb draped over cardboard boxes, a sewing mannequin and globe tumbled together near the window. She pulled the door shut again and climbed downstairs to the main floor.

When not exploring, she was writing. Her first article was on the resources available in Botswana for new missionaries, where English-speaking facilities were available. A second document open was on the food culture, popular dishes and limits on what was available for purchase.

Samantha's fingers flew over the keyboard, her laptop plugged into an outlet alongside an old table lamp. Cross-legged on the sofa, she flipped through piles of saved brochures and training guides from her trip. A CD of conversation Brazilian phrases played in the background to fill up the silence as she wrote. The only other sound was the occasional passing car or the ring of the front bell if one of the workmen forgot his key to the basement-level apartment.

Every day the mail dropped through a slot in the door. An experience that still struck her as unique, after years of post office boxes in scattered locations.

She wasn't expecting anything important–just a credit card bill, a student loan statement, the usual

*The Last Christmas Card*

round of junk mail and sales ads. She picked them up from the mat and glanced over them as she sipped orange juice or carried the recycling out to the curb.

As a child, there was a mailbox at the end of the driveway, where she would kick up clouds of dust from the dirt road whenever she pulled the envelopes from inside. Letters for her mother, grocery ads from the local store, a typewritten reminder from the library that their interlibrary loans had arrived. Back when mail was an experience personal and everyday. Not an occasional surprise or a paper destined for the recycling bin.

She could hear the sound of envelopes thumping softly against the wood floor in the foyer and rose from her seat on the sofa. Padding into the hallway barefoot to collect the pile, she slipped on a pair of old sneakers and a sweatshirt jacket, feeling the need for a little fresh air in the process.

*The Last Christmas Card*

Lifting the papers from the floor, Samantha pushed open the door and stepped onto the foyer. Her fingers sorted the mail as she trod towards the paper recycling bin, crushing wet leaves beneath her sneakers on the walkway.

She tossed the ads for deli meat into the bin, along with an ad for the local election. A fresh flurry of leaves stirred on the sidewalk, papery forms tinged red and yellow from the large maple tree in front of the house. She added a magazine notice addressed to the current occupant to the pile, then glanced at the last piece of mail. A letter envelope.

It was a real letter. That was her first thought as she lifted it up to examine it. The handwriting frail, like veins of ink crisscrossed on the yellowed paper. Two stamps in the corner with a military insignia of some kind.

There were water stains on the address, as if

*The Last Christmas Card*

the envelope had been splattered by rain. The paper felt frail in her hands, as if its corners would crumble beneath her touch. The name Private Mac Hyberg in the far corner, a town in Belgium. The name Bette Larsen visible above the street and city in the center. Maybe Bette was the person who lived in the house before her.

The she saw the postmark. December 1947.

How on earth had it ended up in the mail? For a moment, she was dumbstruck at the thought. Had it accidentally gotten mixed up with the paper? The envelope was still sealed, as if no one had ever opened it.

It had definitely come from the post office. Somehow, this letter had been caught in time, never finding its destination until now.

Inside the house, she carried it to the kitchen, debating what to do. Returning it would do no good–

*The Last Christmas Card*

not after all these years. She couldn't open it to see if the contents were important; it was a felony to open someone else's mail, wasn't it? Even if the letter was over sixty years old, surely the rules applied.

Maybe there was another way. As she tacked it to the dorm fridge in her apartment with a butterfly magnet, she tried to imagine the lost letter from a soldier somewhere in Europe.

\*\*\*\*\*

"Bette? Bette who?" Mrs. Lindell sounded confused.

"The last person who lived here," answered Samantha, trying to sound helpful. "Your relative. Was the family name Larsen, or something like that?"

*The Last Christmas Card*

"No, it was Granger," Mrs. Lindell answered. "My uncle's family. I'm pretty sure there weren't any Larsens in their family tree."

"What about the people who owned the house before that?" suggested Samantha. "Or did they rent it to somebody maybe?" She tapped the envelope against her hand as she cradled the phone on her shoulder. Through the narrow window, she could see the last few leaves drifting from the branches as the mailman made his rounds through the neighborhood.

"I don't know who owned it before them, I'm afraid," said Mrs. Lindell. "He bought it from somebody about ten years ago, but I don't know the name."

"Can you find out, maybe?" Samantha asked. "I think I found something that belonged to them. A letter. It looks kind of important." While this last part was a slight stretch, she hoped it would rouse her landlady to look up the answer.

"I'll go through his papers and see if I can find it," Mrs. Lindell sighed. "But I'm afraid you may have to just leave whatever it is buried or just toss it out. Probably too late to track down the people who wanted it."

By the time she hung up, Samantha had nothing better than the landlady's promise to look up the address, but nothing to go on. She stared at the envelope, wondering how long it had been since anyone by that name had lived in the house.

Maybe someone from the Granger family had married the Larsens. Maybe the Larsens were the previous owners–and somewhere in their paperwork was a forwarding address for the house's buyer.

Or maybe the neighbors would have the answer. On either side of the brownstone was an nearly-identical building in terms of shape and size.

*The Last Christmas Card*

Both were occupied, but the one on the left was divided into apartments similar to her own building.

The one on the right, however, was still someone's home. There was a slim chance the resident could have been living there for years. That was Samantha's thought as pulled on a yellow rain slicker the next afternoon as rain was drizzling from the overcast skies.

The wet stone beneath her sandals was slippery as she took the steps two at time and rang the bell. Disappointed by the sight of a face scarcely older than her own on the other side.

"Sorry, never heard of the Larsens," said the girl. "My grandma lived here a few years ago, but she died last winter."

"Did either of your parents live here?" asked Samantha. Wondering if maybe another relative in the house would remember an older neighbor. "Did they know your grandmother's friends?"

The girl shook her head. "My dad moved in before she died, but he's gone a lot on business trips. I'm just house-sitting for him this weekend. He never talked about anyone coming by while she was sick." The girl was leaning on the door, prepared to close it as soon as possible.

"Well, thanks anyway," Samantha answered. A moment later, a green-painted door was between herself and her neighbor.

Back inside her own apartment, she stared at the envelope propped against the napkin holder on her counter. Wondering if the effort of looking for this person was worth it. After all, her landlady seemed convinced that the former occupants of the house were beyond reach. And perhaps what was inside wasn't so important after all.

As if by impulse, she lifted it and turned it

*The Last Christmas Card*

over, holding the envelope's flap above the steam rising from the tea kettle. The slow puffs enveloped the paper.

*Are you crazy? This isn't yours to open.* The thought popped into her head as the flap lifted from the moisture. She pulled open the drawer to find a glue stick and reseal it. But the object inside caught her eye.

What if the answer to the owner's whereabouts was in this envelope? Her fingers touched the contents, drew them out slowly, afraid of tearing the fragile paper.

A blue and white Christmas card, small and folded to fit the envelope's pocket. A snow-covered village, the steeple of a church and buildings that reminded her of European towns. A white and gold star blazed in one corner above golden swirling letters spelling a message in a foreign language.

She unfolded the card, the inside crammed

*The Last Christmas Card*

with lines written in wavering ink.

*Dear Bets,* it said. *I hope you're reading this somewhere alone before Christmas and that you're having a swell time. I'll bet you've been too busy to write many letters with all the studying for exams. I hope you do the best in your class. Your mama will be proud of you and you'll be a graduate by the time I get back from this war.*

*I carry your photo everywhere I go. I guess I think about you all the time, even when it seems like home is a million miles away and I'll never get back there. It must be Christmas that makes it feel this way. Sometimes I picture you putting tinsel on the tree and wrapping up presents in newspaper. I wanted to get you something special, but there's not much for a soldier to buy where I am right now. I wish I could tell you about it, but the war department wouldn't let me send this if I did.*

*The Last Christmas Card*

*Do you think about me? The last time I saw you, I told you how I felt. If there's a chance you'll still feel the same when the war's over, then tell me so. Tell me you'll keep waiting until I make it back. That way I'll have something to hold onto.*
*Merry Christmas, Bets.*

*Love, Mac.*

Samantha refolded the card and slid it gently into the envelope again. That message from so long ago had never reached its destination. Had he received a letter from his sweetheart, even though this card had disappeared between Europe and home? The long-ago words of the soldier vibrated through her mind like a chord of music echoing after a symphony's end.

Gently, she closed the flap. On the back she read the names of the long-ago Bette Larsen and her sweetheart. Private Mac Hydberg, from the 43rd unit of the Armed Forces. A soldier from somewhere in Boston, Massachusetts.

Even if the Larsen family was hard to find, surely somewhere there was a record of Private Mac Hydberg.

*****

Tyler Lars kept the television on all night. The comforting, dull murmur of voices and noise in the background, the constant static of white noise when the reception gave out. Otherwise, he would hear only the noises in his dreams. The sound of artillery, the explosion of bombs he couldn't diffuse. The screams of children whose parents died in a spray of shrapnel

*The Last Christmas Card*

and heat.

He would jerk awake again, sweating as if the heat of the Iraqi desert surrounded him. Only it was the dimly lit apartment he called home, the worn suede sofa and glow of the electronic clock on the nearby table. The television screen was black; probably from a few seconds of power outage.

Sitting up, he rubbed his leg beneath the blanket. Feeling the familiar ache from the wound torn through flesh and muscle, the twisted scar where a piece of his leg was now missing. The army doctors had done their best to remove every last piece, but sometimes it felt as if heated metal was still embedded in his body. Searing him with the pain as the bodies of fellow soldiers and civilians lay around him.

He crawled from beneath the throw, stumbling over the sneakers piled beside the sofa, the half-eaten microwave dinner still in its tray. Limping towards the

*The Last Christmas Card*

kitchen, he opened the cabinet and rummaged for a bottle of painkillers. Popping two without hesitation, his glance roving towards the postcard pinned to one of the cabinets. Jesus delivering the Sermon on the Mount: a parting gift from the chaplain who sat by his bedside and helped him through the first few weeks of painful recovery.

These days, his faith seemed like the family he never had: absent on all counts. Like the transitional curse of being a foster kid manifested itself in every level of his existence. First his childhood, then his military career, and finally, his God.

He took a long sip from a can of flat soda on the counter, then moved towards the sofa again. The short walk had loosened his cramped muscles and almost hid the limp that confined him to a desk job these days. The worst fate for a serviceman who spent years training to save lives by diffusing explosives–

short of the fate suffered by everyone else the day his patrol stumbled on an unexpected land mine.

If someone asked him what he wished for most in the world, it would be to rewind time and prevent that day from ever happening. As for the rest, he wouldn't trade anything for those days in the service. When he had a sense of comradeship and family he would probably never know again. That was his world; an existence taken away in a matter of minutes, leaving him stuck between military and civilian life in Connecticut.

There was no way he was going to make that transition happen, either.

He ran his fingers through close-shorn sandy hair and glanced towards the mirror. Where a haggard, closed face was visible, surrounded by blond stubble and dark circles from only a few hours of sleep per night.

*The Last Christmas Card*

"Two more hours to go," he muttered, sinking onto the sofa again. As the digital clock registered five a.m.

*****

The handicapped entrance to the Veterans Affairs building was a long walk after a short night's sleep. Tyler pulled open the door and shuffled towards his desk, ignoring the handful of workers armed with military files. He paused only before the wall of fallen heroes. A mosaic of lost officers against a background of the flag.

There was nothing personal at his desk, except himself. A pile of paperwork threatened to topple over as he plopped down in his chair.

*The Last Christmas Card*

"Good weekend, Ty?" a young uniformed woman gave him a smile as she passed by.

"Fine," he answered. Unable to muster more than a brief upward movement of his lips. Somehow he lacked enthusiasm for friendliness in a world of strangers. Even smiling strangers in uniform.

He propped his sore leg on an open desk drawer, rubbing it mechanically as he flipped through a stack of request forms and unfinished reports. When the phone rang, he lifted the receiver. "Veteran's Affairs, this is Sergeant Lars. How may I help you?"

It was the same old line as always. His voice a trifle more tired, all the more businesslike in his opinion. As he looked up medical records, mediated with hospitals and rehabilitation centers, aided family members in the long and winding process of applying for medals or military honors.

"Hi, can you look up a name for me? An

address I mean–for a military member in World War II?"

The voice on the other end was female, possibly young. With a sigh, Tyler shifted his weight impatiently.

"Can I have your name, Ma'am?" he began. There was a slight pause on the other end.

"Samantha Sowerman," the voice replied. "I'm calling about a Private Mac Hydberg. He was from Massachusetts, stationed somewhere in Belgium in 1947–"

"Is he a relative, Ma'am? Or is this call on behalf of an agency involved in Private Hydberg's medical history?" He tapped a pencil against his desk.

"Oh, no. I don't know him." The voice on the other end sounded confused. "I have something that belongs to him. A letter that he mailed when he was stationed overseas. I think it's really important and I

*The Last Christmas Card*

want to talk to him about it, maybe return it to him ...but I guess there might be more than one guy with that name."

He could tell from her tone that she just now considered this possibility. "Ma'am, I can't give you that information without an official reason," he said. "Military personnel addresses aren't handed out on a bulk list to the public..."

"It's a Private Mac Hydberg from Boston, Massachusetts," she repeated, pleadingly. "Please, it's really important. If you could just see if there's a current address for someone with that name, I would be incredibly grateful."

Almost automatically, his fingers had typed the name Hydberg, Mac into the system. Row after row of names identical or similar appeared on the screen, even after he altered the search parameter by year. Most were marked 'deceased'.

*The Last Christmas Card*

"Nineteen forty-seven was a long time ago," he said. "You realize that the soldier whose address you're requesting–"

"Is probably already dead? Yeah, I do, but I want to be sure," persisted the caller.

With a sigh, he drummed his fingers on his desk. He didn't want to give her this information, didn't want to be responsible for breaking the rules and putting some serviceman's name on a list for some senior scam. Why didn't she just find the name online and save him the trouble?

His eye fell on a name in one of the columns. "There's one listed as alive in Cambridge," he said. "And he is a World War II veteran. I'm afraid that most of the list is deceased, ma'am."

"In Cambridge? Okay, that'll help." The female voice sounded brighter. "Thanks."

"You're welcome," he answered, somewhat

gruffly. He hoped she was planning to hang up now and leave him alone in the future. Maybe a try a search engine and realize just how fruitless her search really was.

When he placed the phone in the receiver, he saw the mistake on the screen. The Cambridge address for a Mark Hydberg–next to a deceased Mac Hydberg from Boston.

Scowling, he closed the program window and rubbed his tired eyes. She probably wouldn't even bother to contact this guy. It probably didn't matter that it was the wrong soldier. It was possible she didn't even have the right name, since all she had was a letter from the guy.

He pulled a bottle of aspirin from his desk drawer and popped it open. If he took one now, the muscle soreness would disappear for a little while and he wouldn't have to think about morning patrol or the

*The Last Christmas Card*

faces of the fellow soldiers erased from his unit in a split second.

\*\*\*\*\*

An M. Hydberg was listed in the Cambridge yellow pages. Samantha circled it and his address as she propped her feet on the bus seat in front of her. A long ride on a morning she should be finishing her articles for *Global Outreach.* At least her work wasn't due for another two weeks, giving her time to track down the card's original sender. Maybe he had some idea what happened to Bette Larsen.

The former soldier's home was crammed between an apartment building and a social services office. Scraggly shrubs trimmed in a moth-eaten fashion on either side of the home's concrete steps, shaded by a worn green awning. She rapped on the glass storm door and waited for a response. Her heart was hammering, although the chances that Mac Hydberg would answer were slim. Probably a caretaker or assisted living nurse was here.

After a long wait, the door opened slightly. A frail man in a faded shirt, oxygen lines traveling from his face to a tank beside him.

"Mr. Hydberg?" she asked. The man nodded, a deep frown on his face.

"Do I know you?" his voice trembled slightly. "The agency said they were sending somebody new..."

"Actually, I think I have something that belongs to you. Well, used to belong to you," she interrupted. "Um, can I come inside?"

He drew open the door and let her step into the living room. An untidy pile of newspapers on the floor beside a recliner, a television tuned to a game show. She could smell toast and burned coffee from the kitchen, the strong scent of tuna fish. A shaggy dog pricked up its ears from its curled-up position near the window.

"That's Jip. He won't hurt anyone." Mr. Hydberg closed the door behind her. "Have a cup of coffee, if you want one. Still some in the pot." He shuffled towards the kitchen as Samantha followed.

Trembling hands poured the contents of a percolator into two mismatched cups, as Samantha watched from her seat at the scrubbed kitchen table. Instinctively, she reached to do it for him, then thought better of it. Noticing the quiet dignity with which dishes were stacked on the counter, the rows of canned food beside the stove.

"I guess you didn't find that library book I lost," he chuckled. "Must've left the thing on a bus somewhere. Reckon I'll have to pay the fine after all."

Fishing through her bag, Samantha pulled the worn envelope from inside. Carefully, she held it out.

"Is this the card you mailed when you were stationed overseas?" she asked. "To Bette Larsen?"

He paused, a spoon and creamer container in his hands. A funny look appeared on his face, as if he didn't understand her words. Setting both things slowly on the table, he took the envelope in hand.

"Bette who?" he said. "I didn't know anybody named Bette when I was in the service. A Betty or two, maybe, and a Lisbette..." He trailed off, looking at the postmark in the envelope's corner, the faded writing on the paper.

Fumbling with his glasses, he slid them on. "Private Mac Hydberg," he read aloud. "Now see, that's not me. I never went by Mac, no sir. Went by Mark my whole life."

*The Last Christmas Card*

"Mark?" she repeated. "But the officer at the veteran's office said you were listed as Mac."

"Well, he made a mistake," answered Mr. Hydberg. "My commander never called me anything but Sergeant Mark Hydberg." He handed her the envelope again.

"I know this seems crazy," she said, blushing. "I'm really sorry I bothered you. It's just ... this came to my house a few days ago. Somehow it got lost in the mail for sixty years. And I just wanted the right person to have it."

"Sixty years," he said, softly. "Well, isn't that something." His fingers fumbled with a sugar packet, dumped it into one of the cups before pushing the little basin of packets towards her own cup.

"I wrote to a Maggie when I was in the war," he said. "Maggie Blythe. We were steady all through high school. Gave her my ring and told her that I was

*The Last Christmas Card*

happy to get married when I got back."

Samantha tore open a sugar pack and stirred it into her coffee, the acrid liquid smelling of scorched grounds in the bottom of the pot. "So did she wait for you?" she asked.

"Nope," he answered. "She wrote awhile, then started sending fewer and fewer letters. There was something in her words that didn't feel right. I didn't know what, but no matter how hard I tried, I couldn't fix it."

He took a sip of his coffee. "Turns out she was seeing a boy back home. Got sent home wounded a few weeks after I shipped out. Kind of a hometown hero."

For a moment, he was quiet. "Guess the medals meant more to her than the waiting," he said. "When I got home, she was already married. Somebody sent me a clipping from the newspaper. She told me in her last letter when I was overseas, then never wrote again."

"I'm sorry," said Samantha. "I didn't mean to bring up the past like this..."

He chuckled. "Yeah, you did, toting around that card to find its owner. Nothing but the past in that."

She laughed, softly. "I guess you're right," she answered. "I didn't think of it that way. Too caught up in the search for Bette."

Another moment of silence passed, as Mr. Hydberg swallowed the contents of his coffee cup, fumbling a little so the lukewarm liquid splashed into the saucer. He nodded pleasantly as Samantha commented on the framed postcard on the wall, the twining potato vine kept well-watered by the sink.

As he rose and put his cup in the sink, his brow wrinkled with concentration. "Mac Hydberg," he repeated. "Seems I might've met somebody in the

*The Last Christmas Card*

service with that name. Maybe when I was first stationed overseas. Thought we might be cousins or something."

"I guess there's no chance you saw him when you came back to Massachusetts," ventured Samantha. "Maybe in Boston?"

Mr. Hydberg laughed. "Afraid I don't remember," he said. He reached for Samantha's empty cup, pausing to awkwardly pat her hand.

"Good luck with your search, missy. I hope that card's owner has a happier story than mine."

"Thank you," she answered. The front buzzer sounded as she tucked the card into her bag again.

"That'd be the nurse from the agency," he said. "Come to help with my therapy." He pushed the tank along as he shuffled towards the front door.

"I should go," said Samantha, pushing her chair back from the table and following. "You've been so kind. I'm so sorry I bothered you for no reason."

"You didn't bother me with nothing," he answered. "Nice to see a young face now and then. Somebody who doesn't think the past is all dead history, either."

She thought about his words on the bus home, as she studied the worn envelope from the mail. Wondering if Bette Larsen would care as little about this Christmas card as Maggie Blythe did when she was still writing her soldier. There was a chance that even if she found Bette or Mac, they might toss it aside with indifference. If she ever found them, that is.

As she carefully stroked the yellowed paper, one thought kept popping into her head that had nothing to do with Mac or Bette and their forgotten connection. It had everything to do with the brusque voice who gave her the wrong name and address over the phone.

*The Last Christmas Card*

\*\*\*\*\*

Ty reheated the leftover fish sticks in his refrigerator. The same ones from last night, but it didn't matter to him since it was a fast meal that didn't require thought. He pulled a bottle of pickles from the fridge and limped towards the bread drawer.

The sound of the phone ringing in the living room made him hesitate. Nobody called him unless it was work-related. Setting the jar on the counter, he moved towards the sound. Ignoring the stiffness in his leg as he rested one hand on the table, the other on the receiver.

"Ty here," he said.

"Sergeant Lars, right?" The voice on the other

end sounded slightly familiar. "I looked you up in the phone book and I assume you're the same one who works in Veteran's Affairs."

He recognized the voice by now. The girl with the letter.

"Look, Ms.–" he hesitated, trying to remember the name, "Ma'am, I'm sorry that I gave you the wrong address..."

"Not the wrong address, the wrong person," the voice corrected him. "When I showed up on his doorstep, I felt like an idiot. A complete stranger pestering him about a letter he never even wrote."

She had actually gone to Cambridge to meet this guy? He was floored by the idea. At the most, he thought she would phone someone, not show up for a face-to-face meeting.

"And it's Samantha Sowerman, by the way," she added, after a moment.

*The Last Christmas Card*

"I'm sorry," he repeated. "If you want, Miss Sowerman, I can—"

"Frankly, I'm not sure I should ask for your help again," she laughed. "I mean, the last time I ended up meeting the wrong person in Cambridge, so I might be better off on my own."

He let silence occupy the line while he rubbed his sore leg. Guilt crept through his veins like a virus over his mistake. He owed her something to make up for it; when he was at his best in his unit, he never cut corners and never let anyone down like this.

"Maybe there's something I can do," he said. "If I understood what was so important about this letter you have ... then I could figure out how to find its sender." Now if this was some kind of scam, maybe he would scare her away. If not, then maybe he would find an answer to her problem.

"You're in Connecticut, right?" Samantha

Sowerman asked. "That's not that far for me to come. If I met you, I could explain it better, I think."

Met him? Was she crazy? He wondered where on earth this person was that she planned to drop by and tell him some crazy story about a letter she found.

"You could come by my office if you want," he began.

"I think there's probably a cafe near the bus station," she said. "I could meet you there for lunch if you're free around one or so."

"Do you work nearby, Ma'am?" he asked.

"No, but I have plenty of time," she answered. "It's not a problem for me to meet if it's not for you."

This was crazy. And weird. But he felt he owed her this after his mistake. The kind of carelessness he wouldn't have allowed in the past.

"All right, fine," he said. "If you'll tell me which one it is, I'll be there around twelve forty-five."

*The Last Christmas Card*

"I'll call you back." Samantha's voice sounded more cheerful now. He heard a click and the sound of a dial tone. She was gone and he was committed to having lunch with a total stranger in search of another stranger.

Almost as crazy as going to a total stranger's house over an old letter.

\*\*\*\*\*

There were only two other people in the cafe as Samantha sat in the corner booth thumbing through her Bible. A man sat at the counter chomping into a sandwich, while a college boy chatted on a cell phone at a window table.

The next customer who entered wore a faded

jacket with a military emblem on the sleeve. A pair of jeans and worn sneakers, hair close-cropped to reveal a short scar traveling along his temple.

When he spotted her, he crossed the room with a firm stride that favored his left leg. Pausing with a slight smile when he reached her table.

"Miss Sowerman?" he asked. She nodded.

"You must be Sergeant Lars," she said, closing the leather cover and placing it aside. "I'm Samantha." She held out her hand.

He shook it, then slid into the booth across from her. "I guess I was expecting someone a little ... older." She wondered why he said that, since the only notable thing about their phone conversation was her persistence. Perhaps it was to cover for the fact that, despite her semi-shabby casual attire–a camp t-shirt, a pair of khakis–he kept staring at her. As if he found something striking about her corkscrew blond hair and

*The Last Christmas Card*

clear complexion.

"Maybe you expected me to be older because I'm asking you about somebody from World War II," she said, with a smile. "I know it may seem a little odd, but it's important. That's why I'm trying to find him."

She pulled a piece of paper from her bag. "This is it," she said. "It's a card, actually. I know, because I steamed it open." With a blush as she admitted this.

He took hold of the envelope and studied it. A yellowed piece of paper with colored stamps and cursive letters forming the address. The flap was partly open, so he lifted the edge and pulled the card from inside. A blue and white folded sheet.

She watched his face as he read it, studying his haggard features, the curve of his jaw. He was still young, but there was something old in his attitude. A look of sadness in his face even when he smiled. Right now, his expression was serious as he gazed at the lines on the paper. The lines around his mouth softened as he carefully folded it again.

"See what I mean?" she said. "I want the right person to read those words. I know they're supposed to be private–that I wasn't supposed to open it. It was meant for whoever lived in my house sixty years ago."

"So you found this in your house," he said. She shook her head.

"No, it was delivered. By the Post Office," she added. "A couple of days ago."

He raised his eyebrows. "They put this through the slot with the rest of your mail? After all these years?"

She shrugged. "These things happen. Envelopes fall through the cracks, get discovered again. You read about it on the internet all the time. The important part is, it came to me and I'm going to find its owner."

"But its owner is Bette Larsen," he pointed out. "Not the soldier who mailed it."

She shrugged. "I'm trying to find the Larsens, but it's not exactly working out. Apparently, they haven't lived in this house for ages. The current owner hasn't even heard of them."

Releasing a long sigh, he slid the envelope in front of her. "How long have you been living in the house?" he asked. "Long enough to look for any clues to the former owner's identity? Go through the closets and shelves and the like?"

"Only a week," she answered. "I'm just there temporarily. Between projects, since I finished my last mission trip."

"You're a missionary?" He glanced towards the Bible at her elbow. Before she could reply, the waitress approached with a pad and pencil.

"You two ready to order?" she asked.

"Just a turkey sandwich and chips, please," said Samantha. Her companion glanced over the menu briefly, taking in the list of items.

"Burger and fries," he answered. "Hold the ketchup, please. Just water to drink." He cleared his throat and reached for the napkin holder.

"Are you a believer?" The suddenness of Samantha's question took him by surprise. He paused for a moment, then shrugged his shoulders.

"Sort of," he answered. "I used to be. Sometimes life makes it hard to keep on, that's all."

"You were overseas, weren't you?" she said. "You were in the war."

He chuckled. "Yeah, that's right. How'd you know?" He patted his thigh with one hand. "Did my stiff knee give me away?"

The grin illuminated his face, transforming the

lines of pain with a sudden glimpse of warmth. He ran his fingers through the sandy hair trimmed close to his head, telling her the pain in his leg was a sensitive issue.

"Actually, it was what you said about your faith," she answered. "See, I've met former soldiers before. On mission trips and when I was working in villages. They told me that war either drives you away from God or pulls you to Him."

She flipped open her Bible, turning the pages a few times before she drew something from inside. "That was T.J. He became a medical missionary pilot after his time in Afghanistan was up. He used to talk about what it was like to see women and children killed in village raids. To see children forced into battle by radical ideology or fear." She held up the snapshot of a dark-skinned man in camouflage and denim, one hand resting on a light aircraft.

*The Last Christmas Card*

"I was in Iraq," Ty answered, after a moment. "Bomb squad. Five years of training and service until I ended up here." His voice tightened slightly.

"What happened?" Samantha tucked the photo in her Bible again. As she looked into his face, she regretted asking the question. The grin vanished, the momentary softness in his face replaced by something cold and hard.

"There was a land mine buried outside a village," he answered. "We found it the hard way. Three civilians, two soldiers, and me. Only two of us were lucky in the end."

The waitress slid their orders from her tray, along with a paper-wrapped straw. Ty lifted his glass and took a long sip, his eyes fixed on a point away from Sam and the waitress, taking in the scattered customers and grey scene outside the cafe windows.

A sudden warmth on his hand made him glance

*The Last Christmas Card*

down to see Samantha's fingers touching his own.

"I'm sorry," she said, gently. "I shouldn't have asked. I'm kind of ... blunt sometimes. I forget that not everybody wants to say what's on their mind."

She half-expected him to draw back, but he didn't. For a moment, his hand lingered under hers, before he removed his fingers. Gently, however, as if he was afraid of hurting her.

"Well, that's the past," he said. "Now I work behind a desk. Looking up addresses for people who have plenty of spare time for returning lost letters." He tucked a napkin in his lap and reached for a fry on his plate. "Up until now, I assumed this was some kind of family thing. Maybe a lost grandfather or great-uncle. Maybe a big will or inheritance involved." With a subtle wink that revealed he was kidding.

She chewed a bite of her sandwich. "Nope," she said. "Just a concerned citizen. No family left to

*The Last Christmas Card*

give me anything more than a Christmas card." Waving the envelope as proof before sliding it off the table, away from the condiment bottles between them.

Across from her, he took another bite from his burger, using a napkin to swipe a smear of mustard from his jacket sleeve. The fabric so battered she wondered if it had seen more than one tour of duty. Had his family been military, too?

"Is your family all in the service?" she asked.

"No," he answered. "No family. Just me."

His brusque tone stung slightly; she bit her lip and glance down at the table to avoid letting him see that. Until now, she had been tempted to ask him more about his life. Something she would skip, since she sensed that he didn't feel the urge to explain.

Crumbling his napkin, he tossed it next to his half-eaten burger. "Look, there's a lot of names in the database, but he's in there somewhere," he said. "I'll

*The Last Christmas Card*

see what I can do about finding Private Hydberg for you."

"You will?" Her voice betrayed surprise. "I thought you didn't believe in this."

He shrugged. "I just thought you could use a hand. Since it's so important to you to find a home for that card." Pulling his wallet from his pocket, he tossed a card in front of her.

"That's my number at the office and my home number below," he said. "In case you're not in reach of a phone book." He pulled a few bills from the wallet and tucked them beneath his food basket.

"I'll call you if I find anything," he said, rising from the booth.

It was a signal their meeting was over; she took the hint and offered him a farewell smile.

"Thanks," she said. Tucking her Bible into her bag, slipping the card he gave her inside its pages.

*The Last Christmas Card*

A step towards the door and he hesitated a moment. "Keep me posted if you find something first," he said.

"So you won't waste your time," she guessed. "Sure, I can do that."

He lingered between the booth and the exit, as if debating his reply.

"Yeah," he said. "Thanks." With that, he pushed open the door and moved stiffly to the sidewalk. Keeping his stride as normal as possible so long as he was in sight of the girl in the booth.

*****

The database for military records was vast, organized by name, date, service, unit, and other pertinent details. This time, Ty was careful with his search parameters.

Hydberg Mac, Private. Massachusetts. The date was harder, since he had no idea what time span Private Hydberg's tour of duty encompassed. He was somewhere in Belgium in 1947–but so were thousands of American soldiers.

The screen spit out a long list of matches. More than enough were exact, more than enough were deceased. He repressed a groan as he scrolled through the names, looking at the possibilities. Printing off a list of candidates, he watched as the printer issued page after page.

This would mean hours of work, probably making phone calls and contacting veteran's hospitals. The kind of thing he already wanted to escape, only now he was doing it without pay and without any kind of reward–except maybe a smile of thanks from the girl with the Christmas card.

Samantha Sowerman. For some reason he kept thinking about her even as his phone remained silent except for business calls. There was something about her that made him curious. That made him long for something just out of reach. She reminded him of things he never had, of things he wanted to have, but had no proof that she was any of those things.

Didn't she say she had no family? That she moved around a lot? How was that any different from the life he had always known? The only difference between them was her faith. Rock solid while his was sliding like gravel towards the canyon below.

He couldn't put his finger on it, but it was definitely there. Even if it was just his imagination making reality out of nothing.

Releasing a long breath, he worked a pencil over the names, crossing off the least likely candidates with imperfect name matches. The ones who returned to the U.S. before 1947. What was left would require a little more work on his part. As he circled the soldiers who were listed as Boston natives or part of the surrounding community.

He hoped wherever she was, Samantha Sowerman was making better progress than he was.

*****

Weeks passed since Samantha had taken the bus to meet Sergeant Lars in Connecticut. The last of the red leaves from the maple chased each other across the entrance to the brownstone, its exterior cool and damp in the days leading up to Thanksgiving.

Inside, she huddled over a cup of warm tea and

*The Last Christmas Card*

her laptop, proofreading the drafts of her column before mailing them. Remembering her first and only Thanksgiving celebrated in Australia, thousands of miles from her homeland. Someone in their group had molded a turkey out of tofu and stuffed it with a spicy dressing that burned her tongue. A far cry from the holidays of her childhood, her mother's turkey roll and sage dressing.

It was part of the long-past traditions that Samantha remembered from her childhood. Fragments of Christmas trees and cards strung from greenery boughs, of carved pumpkins and patriotic cupcakes in the summertime. The kinds of things she had done without since life on her own.

As she typed, she sniffed the air periodically. The turkey soup on her stove had bubbled over a few minutes before. She wasn't as handy with modern pots and pans as she was with the clay cooking dishes she

*The Last Christmas Card*

handled in the remote villages. Her mother would have wondered how someone could struggle with a saucepan and stove who had spent months cooking over an open flame. Or boiled noodles over a burner using nothing but a tin cup and a pair of unused surgical tongs.

Pinned to her refrigerator, the envelope was visible beneath the butterfly magnet. Over the last few weeks, Samantha had combed through the online phone listings and local phone book, searching for any sign of the Larsen or Hydberg families. Dialing the numbers of strangers in hopes that one would claim Bette Larsen or Mac Hydberg as their own.

"No, sorry, never heard of her," was the response of one man. "I think you have the wrong Larsens."

"Nobody in our family ever went by the name of Mac," said a woman she phoned a few hours later.

"Sorry, this is the Gillis household. Either you have the wrong number or you're trying to call the previous owners." This person hung up before she could ask them anything else.

She was beginning to feel as if these two people and their families disappeared from the planet altogether. Maybe Sergeant Lars was right about this: it was an impossible task.

She had called his desk once or twice out of curiosity, but he was always out. The female officer who answered didn't seem to know where he was most of the time. She left messages, but there was no response.

Once she reached a civilian worker, a chatty girl who enjoyed having something to do besides push paperwork. Happy to discuss anything, even a coworker she had only known for a few months.

"It's kind of sad, actually," she told Samantha.

*The Last Christmas Card*

"I mean, he had such an impressive record of service. They said he was one of the best until his accident. Now he barely comes into work some days."

Samantha bit her lip, unsure how to respond. Were they talking about his muscle pain—or his emotional state? But the girl had moved on to the subject of finding an office email address for Samantha to contact.

When the phone rang in her apartment, Samantha lifted the receiver, expecting the voice of her landlady or maybe one of the neighbors on the other end. She shifted her cup of tea away from the keyboard, to the space beside her bowl of soup.

"Hello?" she said.

"Miss Sowerman, this is Sergeant Lars." At the sound of his voice, she felt a jolt of surprise.

"Did you find something?" she asked. "And it's Samantha. Miss Sowerman sounds kind of strange to me."

She heard a slight cough on the other end that might have been a laugh. "I think I found something for you, Ma'am," he said. "A couple of definite Boston residents who were stationed in Belgium during 1947. Now, they might not be the ones–"

"What are their addresses?" Already her fingers were poised over the keyboard as she waited.

"Well, one is deceased," answered Ty. "But the second is alive in Pennsylvania. An address near the state line, so it's not exactly close to Boston..."

Her fingers typed quickly, even as her mind absorbed the news. She had half-hoped Mac Hydberg was still somewhere in Boston–or at least Massachusetts–so returning the card would be simple.

"I could mail it there, but I want to return it in person," she said, thinking out loud. "I'm supposed to rent a car over Thanksgiving to run some errands.

*The Last Christmas Card*

Maybe then I could ..."

"...could drop by and hand it over," finished Sergeant Lars on the other end.

She couldn't suppress her laugh in response. "Yeah, I guess so," she answered. "I suppose you think I'm crazy for wanting to do this face-to-face."

"I didn't say crazy," he said. "The easy way would be to pop it in an envelope and hope for the best. But I suppose you want to be dead certain before you hand it over."

She thought she detected a slight note of bitterness in his voice. His good humor vanished quickly, she couldn't help but notice. Like a flock of birds startled from a tree, leaving the branches and trunk bare of life.

"Well, anyway, thanks for helping, Sergeant," she answered. "If I make contact with them, I'll let you know. If you want."

*The Last Christmas Card*

"Sure," he answered. His voice sounded faraway now. "Here's hoping it's the right one."

When she hung up the phone, she studied the address intently. It was a long distance to travel simply to return a lost card. Ty had informed her their phone number was unlisted, otherwise she could contact them in advance. As it was, maybe she was better off sending a letter than taking off for the Pennsylvania border to drop in on total strangers.

But where was the adventure in that? Surely a card delayed for sixty years deserved a better delivery into the hands that may have been waiting a lifetime for it.

\*\*\*\*\*

*The Last Christmas Card*

She was definitely crazy for doing this. But there was no better way, she decided. As she straightened the collar of her best shirt above her only non-holey sweater and checked her reflection in the rear view mirror.

The day after Thanksgiving, Samantha had rented a car and driven outside of Boston to help an old friend pack her things for a cross-country move. Originally she had planned to drive to the coast for a few days, but plans change. With a Christian rock cd blasting from the speakers and a road map unfolded on the seat beside her, she wound her ways towards the Pennsylvania border.

She pulled onto the street of the Hydberg house on Saturday morning and parked on the neighborhood curb. Old trees filled the front yard of the home, marked with white gingerbread trim and dark green nandina and holly bushes bursting with red berries along the neighboring fence. She felt hesitant about actually walking up to the front door and ringing the bell. Reaching for her shoulder bag, the envelope protruding from the outside pocket.

As she walked up the sidewalk, she spotted a figure approaching from the opposite direction, slamming shut the door of a small car with military plates. There was something familiar about their stride, even at this distance. Something too familiar.

"Sergeant Lars?" She slowed, staring at him as he approached. "What are you doing here?"

"The same thing you are," he answered. "Seeing if this is the right place." A half-smile crept across his face as he opened the gate.

"I don't understand." Confusion crept into her voice for her reply. "I mean, you didn't believe in this...you never said anything over the phone about coming here ..."

*The Last Christmas Card*

He shrugged his shoulders, his arm steering her through the gate before he closed it behind them. "I just thought I'd check them out for you."

"But you knew I was coming here," she protested, as she climbed the steps. "Anyway, you knew I was thinking about it—"

"Look, are you offended that I came?" For a moment, his smile disappeared as he paused halfway up the house steps. Samantha blushed, realizing the way her protests sounded. Like a child whose ball was stolen by a neighborhood kid.

"No," she stammered, a rush of dismay sweeping over her at the thought of hurting him with those words. "Not at all. I'm just ... surprised, that's all."

He didn't say anything as he knocked on the door. The rap was sharp against the carved panels, an etched glass window occupying the upper half. She could see the smoky outline of a face on the other side, peering through the glass before opening the door.

"Can I help you?" The man on the other side of the threshold smiled cheerfully, middle-age lines stretched into warm creases.

"Yes, actually," said Ty. "Is Mac Hydberg here? Private Mac Hydberg of the U.S. Army?"

The smile on the man's face dimmed slightly. "You mean my grandfather," he said. "He's not anymore, I'm afraid. He's been in a nursing home these past two months." He glanced from Ty to Samantha and back again.

"Are you two here to see him?" he asked.

"We wanted to ask him a question," Samantha said. "About whether he knew a Bette Larsen and whether–" she drew the envelope from her bag, "–he mailed her this."

The man turned the envelope over in his hand,

studying the address. "Why don't you two come in?" he asked, opening the door wider.

"Hey, honey, we have a couple of guests," he called. "I'm Nate Hydberg, by the way." He gestured towards a woman emerging from the kitchen wearing a holiday sweater and apron. "This is my wife Janet. My dad–Mac junior–is out back with the rest of the family."

"I'm sorry–are we interrupting something?" asked Ty, his brow furrowed. "Stupidly, I was thinking with Thanksgiving past, that now was a good time to drop by."

"Oh, it's just a little family thing," Janet answered. "It's fine, sit down." She patted the sofa cushions and motioned for Samantha to sit.

"Where are those albums of Grandpa's, honey?" asked Nathan, scanning the crowded bookshelves in the room. After a moment, he pulled a thick scrapbook from among the paperbacks and photograph albums crammed around it.

"This has some of Grandpa's old pictures in it," he said. "From before he went overseas. Friends, family, a few of his fellow soldiers are in here, too." He handed Samantha the album as he sank down in a nearby armchair.

Samantha opened the volume, revealing black photo pages with snapshots clipped inside. Black and white images of women in flowered dresses and chiffon, men in double-breasted suits and fedoras.

"That's Mac Hydberg the original." Nathan sat forward in his chair to tap a photo in the corner of the page. "That's my future Grandma, Elise Howard."

"So not Bette Larsen, huh?" said Ty. Sitting next to Samantha, he drew closer to study the picture. His breath brushed against her skin, his hand mere inches from her own as he took hold of the book and

*The Last Christmas Card*

drew it closer.

"I don't recall Grandpa ever mentioning a girl named Bette," admitted Nathan. "He used to tell stories about old girlfriends before he went off to war. But by the time he was drafted, he claimed he was in love with his future wife. I guess maybe there could have been a secret love or an old flame," Nathan laughed.

In between the photos were mementos of the past: party invitations, flyers for town events, even a flattened bottle cap glued to the page. As she turned through the volume, Samantha looked for any samples of handwriting that matched the envelope. The curving loops above the photos on the pages seemed almost feminine by comparison. Mac's daughter or wife probably assembled this volume for him. Writing "Mac and his mother Ethel, 1944" and "Friends Frank and Julie, 1948".

*The Last Christmas Card*

She wondered if any of the faces belonged to Bette Larsen. Would he keep a snapshot of a girl he begged to love him from far overseas? Especially if it wasn't returned as he wished?

"Didn't your grandfather have a girlfriend who died while he was in the war?" asked Janet. "I seem to remember him telling the story once. About a sister of one of his friends, maybe. She died of the flu or pneumonia."

"Maybe so," Nathan answered, slowly. "Dad would know–honey, see if he'll come inside for a few minutes."

Janet opened one of the glass patio doors and stepped outside. The brief sound of laughter and voices talking, the smell of food cooking before the door closed again.

"So how did you end up with this card?" asked Nathan, picking up the envelope again from the table.

*The Last Christmas Card*

"It was delivered to my house," answered Samantha. "Sixty years late, I guess."

His mouth twisted into an incredulous smile as he glanced at the address on the envelope. "You drove all the way from Boston to find out who sent a card?" he asked.

"Yeah, she did," Ty answered. "Apparently, we're kind of crazy like that."

Something about his "we" made her blush. A sense of comradeship between them that she hadn't felt when he told her he would help. Picturing the man beside her as doing crazy things seemed impossible–even knowing his past. But a man who once diffused bombs would hardly consider delivering mail to a stranger an obstacle.

"You're planning to give this card back to Bette, I take it?" asked Nathan. "That's why you wanted to see Grandpa."

*The Last Christmas Card*

"It is," said Samantha. "Do you think there's any chance he would remember her? If he knew her, that is?" She crossed her fingers that the answer was yes. But the face across from her looked gloomy.

"Probably not," Nathan answered, gently. "He's on a lot of medication since his hip surgery is scheduled for a couple of days from now. His car accident left him in a lot of pain–he hasn't even recognized me the last few times I visited." Nathan fingered the seal on the envelope, as if curious about what was inside. Glancing up, he smiled at the sight of a man opening the patio door.

"Here's Dad," he announced. "Dad, these people think they found a card that Grandpa mailed during the war. To an old girlfriend, maybe."

Mac Junior shrugged off his heavy parka and gave them a grin. "Friends of my father, eh?" he asked. "Come to look through all his old pictures–must be a dozen albums on those shelves."

"Does this look like something he would've mailed?" Nathan handed his father the card.

Fumbling through his pocket, Mac produced a pair of reading glasses and studied the envelope carefully. He turned it over, examining the sealed flap, then back again. One finger traced the postmark, then the address in the center.

"No," he said. "That's not my father's handwriting. He always crossed his 't's funny–that's how I always recognized his papers. And I think he was stationed in England by '47. Almost home again, so to speak."

Samantha's face fell with disappointment. Mac handed the card to her. "Sorry about that," he said. "Shame it's not my dad's, though. We might've been able to find her since he kept a pretty thorough photographic record of his girlfriends." He sat down on the love seat. "Some pretty girls in that album. Not as pretty as yours, though," he said to Ty with a wink in Samantha's direction.

Ty's face reddened for a moment. "I'm not– she's ... I'm afraid I'm not that lucky, sir. Just a friend." He glanced apologetically towards Samantha as a crimson flush crept upwards from his collar.

"That's too bad," laughed Mac. "If I were you, I'd do something about that before she finds some other young fellow."

Nathan checked his watch. "We'd like for you to join us for dinner if you like. We're grilling a couple of turkeys, having some salad and trimmings. Late Thanksgiving, since Grandpa's condition was touch and go until now."

"Oh, no, we couldn't impose on you like that," Samantha answered, closing the photo album.

"It's no imposition," answered Janet. "We'd be

honored."

Samantha noticed the woman's glance falling on the faded military insignia on Ty's sleeve, where his military service was quietly displayed. "Then we'll stay," she said, glancing at Ty's face to gauge his reaction. "Won't we?"

He was quiet for a moment. "Sure," he answered, finally. "Sounds great."

"Then I'll go set a couple of extra places," said Janet, her face brightening.

*****

The swing in the Hydberg's backyard was suspended from a large oak tree. Samantha pushed herself back and forth, her sneakers trailing in the dust circle beneath. No doubt created by the great-grandchildren of Mac Hydberg as they pushed themselves higher.

    Smoke drifted from the grill as the fire cooled in the late afternoon. She could still taste the smoky flavor of the meat, the onion stuffing and macaroni salad from Janet's generous servings. The chaos of happy family conversation as a crowd of Hydbergs passed each other dishes and rolls.

    This kind of gathering was more foreign than the countries stamped on her passport; even when her mom was alive, there was no big family to plan holiday gatherings or bring casseroles and pies to the dining table.

    The patio door slid open, the sound of conversation drifting outside as Ty emerged. He closed the door behind him, stuffing his hands in his jacket.

"Kind of cool out here," he said, crossing the patio. "Sure you don't need something better than that old windbreaker?" He nodded towards her jacket.

"I'm warm enough," she answered. "Too much turkey, so I thought I'd try a little fresh air."

With a short laugh, he strolled closer. "They're quite a family," he said, leaning against a plastic playhouse assembled in the yard. "Can't say I'm used to that kind of holiday celebration."

"I remember you said you didn't have any family," she answered.

He dropped his gaze for a moment. "True. I was a foster kid," he answered. "Spent most of childhood moving from house to house. They said it was so we wouldn't get attached. But that's what you want most, then. Something to be attached to."

The toes of her sneakers dug into the dirt. "I didn't have this kind of life as a kid, either," she answered. "My mom and I were pretty much alone. And when she died, there was just me."

His eyes raised to meet hers, a strong blue that she had never noticed until now. "Sucks, doesn't it?" he asked.

She couldn't help the laugh that escaped her. "I guess it does, sometimes," she answered. "Seeing a family like this, all their traditions and connections, it makes you wish you had something like it."

"That would be kind of inconvenient for a missionary, wouldn't it?" he answered. "I mean, cutting those ties again and again, every time you take off for foreign lands."

"Any more than for a soldier?" she retorted. He hesitated, then chuckled.

"True," he said. "Maybe I was lucky to be on my own, huh?" There was a slightly bitter tone in his voice.

*The Last Christmas Card*

She shook her head. "You weren't alone. Maybe you didn't have a family, but someone still cared about you." She glanced towards the house. "Don't you know that's why they asked us to stay today?"

His jaw tightened. "I don't need people to feel sorry for me," he said. "It was a choice I made, a job that I loved–it wasn't something people have to give me gifts for doing."

"That's not why they did it," she answered. "They wanted to say thank you, that's all." She let go of the swing's ropes and stood in front of him.

"Besides, I didn't mean just them," she said. "I was talking about God. You said you used to believe, remember?" She raised her eyebrows defiantly as he looked away.

"It's not that I don't believe," he argued. "It's just ... hard. After everything." He turned away, staring through the glass at the family party inside.

"I didn't mean to sound so harsh about the pity thing," he said, after a moment. "It means a lot. What people like them do for service members. I just don't want anyone to think I'm fishing for sympathy these days." He rubbed his right leg, as if the muscle ached in the cool air.

"I wish they had been the right family," said Samantha. "Maybe there's no chance of finding the right ones. Not everybody has a happy ending and even then–"

"–not everyone has the ending you imagine," he concluded. "Like this one–if they'd been the right family, then Bette Larsen's card wouldn't exactly have any value, would it?"

"I don't know," Samantha answered. "I think that's up to her to decide. Maybe even after all these years, even if she never saw him again, she would still want that piece of her past."

He studied her face intently as she spoke, a faint smile appearing on his own. She couldn't fathom what was deep in those eyes. Pain? Amusement? She didn't know him well enough to be sure of anything.

They were silent together, leaning against the plastic slide that traveled down the playhouse side. The breeze ruffled her curls, lifted the collar of his faded jacket. Both watching the glowing world on the other side of the glass, where Janet was maneuvering past a table crowded with grown-ups and kids making popcorn balls.

He cleared his throat. "I want to keep looking for Private Hydberg," he said. "The right one is out there somewhere. If there's a chance he's alive or has family around, maybe you can still find Bette."

She glanced up at him. "You think they still have a connection?" she asked.

*The Last Christmas Card*

"Why not?" he said. "Maybe it's possible that people who meet are always connected somehow." A trace of the warm smile she had seen before appeared for a moment, then vanished with a brusque sigh.

"Ready to go say goodbye?" he asked, holding out his arm.

"Yeah. Let's go." Sliding her fingers around his sleeve, she felt the warmth between the rough fabric as they walked towards the family inside.

\*\*\*\*\*

Was home a physical place? Samantha had asked herself this question more than once. The collection of postcards from her favorite places in all the world didn't include a photograph of her childhood

*The Last Christmas Card*

home, for instance. The only one she had was a grainy image shot from the middle of the road: a grey blur obscuring half of the house, the limbs of an elm swayed by stormy winds.

To her, home had become a heavenly destination; an earthly place defined by friends and family and the benchmarks in her faith. That was her conclusion after years of traveling across the globe, her earthly possessions confined to a couple of bags and a storage box or two in the attic of a family member.

Now she was rifling through someone else's possessions, looking for a trace of their earthly connections. Opening the brownstone's closets, sorting through boxes of private possessions and forgotten junk left behind when the house was emptied. Old newspapers and magazines, a woman's hat worn through with moth holes.

*The Last Christmas Card*

    She pulled open the drawers in the living room bureau and the old china cabinet covered by sheets and left in the former kitchen. Which in a matter of weeks would be converted into a dining room and guest bedroom for the future tenant of her apartment. In each drawer, she found nothing but dust and peeling contact paper.

    In the attic, she poked around with a broom, searching for old letters or correspondence tucked in the eaves. Prying open mildewed cardboard boxes, she discovered faded old clothes and a complete set of encyclopedias, assorted kitchen wares and old holiday decorations. But no trace of the Larsens, nothing that could be tied to their past. Not even the worn Sunday School Bible found in a jumble of books in the old wardrobe.

    Downstairs, Samantha brewed a cup of tea and flipped through the pile of junk mail from the front mat. Brushing cobwebs from her sleeves and hair periodically, wondering what Tyler Lars would have to say about her desperate search.

When she first met him, she would imagine him calling it a wild goose chase. But now she wasn't sure. Not after he volunteered to continue the search on his own, without her asking for his help.

She wondered what he was doing right now. Was he sitting at his desk, popping painkillers and trying not to think about the soldiers who were killed in his unit. Or was his mind on their conversation from a week ago, when she saw a glimpse of the fragile soul within?

If only she could think of a way to reach him. Somewhere within those depths, his faith was still there. It had kept him alive through tragedy, had made him strong in the face of pain and adversity. If he could only see it; if he could only realize that God had a reason for him to survive the past.

Resting her face in her hands, she prayed silently as her lips moved to the words in her head. *Please, Lord, please change the direction his feet travel. Show him Your light and a new path of service. He's lost right now without the dreams he held onto for so long. Now that it's gone, he needs you more than ever. Show him what you have in store for him before he slips away.*

She opened her eyes, gazing at the laptop screen before her. A picture of her Australian mission building against a brown terrain of wind-swept dirt and crossed fence lines. A little piece of the home she once knew for six months of her life.

Would she feel the same way about Brazil? For once, she tried not to think about the answer as she closed the laptop screen.

*The Last Christmas Card*

\*\*\*\*\*

Finding people who were still alive was hard. Finding people who already died was even harder, Ty discovered. Dialing number after number, trying to locate next of kin or surviving spouses. All to ask a question about a person most of them had never heard of before.

"Most of them" was a generous assessment of reality, actually; half the phones never picked up, still others were answered by relatives clueless about the past of their veteran family member. Some were wrong numbers altogether, the curse of internet phone references and incorrect family links on websites.

He ran his hand over his weary features, one elbow resting on a stack of finished reports. A handful of names were crossed off his list for good. But it didn't look like a happy ending was in store for Samantha's Christmas card.

"Hey, Ty, you're looking good," teased a passing coworker. A crimson flush spread over Ty's face. As if being clean-shaven was a sign his life was improving. Or the presence of a couple of framed photos on his desk made a difference in the pile of papers or the ever-handy aspirin bottle in the top drawer of his desk.

"Thanks," he answered. Less gruffly than usual, aware that it was meant as a compliment. Tugging his sleeves up, he pushed through the list of phone number matches for a Mac Lydberg in Connecticut.

After work, he went for a brief jog. Aware that the pain in his muscle would punish him later, but wanting the excuse to run. It made the memories of

*The Last Christmas Card*

Iraq real again; of the patrols and perimeters, of the smell of the hot desert and the sense of fear as he donned his explosives gear.

Heart pounding, his thoughts flew through those years, into the present. Where he couldn't help but feel the lines of the Christmas card matching the rhythm of his movement with their urgency. Private Mac Hydberg's plea for his sweetheart's answer as war raged all around him.

Did it matter if he found the answer? It seemed to matter a lot to the missionary girl who spent hours riding buses to other states, trying to find the card's owner. It wasn't an obsession; more like a calling with her. As if she couldn't help herself, trying to help others over something as small as a lost letter.

Maybe that was why he couldn't let this go. The girl who believed God wanted her to deliver a long-lost Christmas card.

*The Last Christmas Card*

He couldn't afford to think about that right now, not with his life like it was. He stumbled up the steps to his house, leaning on the pillar for momentary support. Gasping for breath as he felt flames passing through his thigh muscles, reminding him that part of it was forever lost after that day in the desert.

Digging his keys from the pocket of his shorts, he pushed the key into the lock as the December chill bit through his bare skin. Stupid idea, going for a run in workout gear on a day that threatened snow. Even now, he wasn't used to the New England cold, the sudden snowdrifts that appeared on the sidewalk and streets. Not to mention the blizzards that rocked the landscape for days.

Inside, the steam from his radiator saturated his sweat with heat in a matter of minutes. He shrugged off his jacket, limped towards the rows of bottled water on the kitchen counter.

*The Last Christmas Card*

His eye caught a flash of color from the postcard pinned to his cabinet. The memory of the chaplain behind it became vivid for a moment: the sound of a voice reciting a prayer, a hand holding his as he screamed in pain.

Almost like the feel of the missionary girl's hand in the restaurant. The same feeling of warmth and understanding permeating his skin, awakening a sense of connection with a greater being than himself.

He took a long sip from the bottle and closed his eyes. Hanging onto that thought for just a few minutes more before it escaped.

\*\*\*\*\*

Samantha dumped the last handful of torn

*The Last Christmas Card*

newspapers, sticks, and leaves into a plastic garbage bag–the remains of a squirrel's nest constructed in the eaves of the attic. Her exploration had uncovered it when she moved aside a stack of empty cardboard boxes abandoned by the previous resident.

Tying it shut, she took one last glance around her at the attic, as if a secret might suddenly be visible despite her previous searches. Nothing. Only the glint of tinsel protruding from an ornament box, a pile of yarn poking up from an old workbasket of rug patterns.

Hauling the sack into the back courtyard, she stuffed it into a garbage can used by the workers renovating the basement. A pile of old plaster surround the back patio, along with a tangle of dead roses pulled from along the walls.

An old woman shuffled from an open door in the house behind the brownstone. In her hand, a broom

*The Last Christmas Card*

as she made her way towards a little stone area lined with potted plants.

She was a complete stranger to Samantha, who had assumed the silent house behind her own was empty until this moment. She watched the red kerchief bob above a worn silk blouse and linen slacks.

"Is that your garden?" Samantha called. The woman hesitated for a moment, then looked in her direction.

"It is," she answered, her voice frail with age. "All I can keep up with at my age. But once this whole back lot was a garden, when I was a girl. Then I grew a Victory Garden–do you know what that is?"

A shiver ran down Samantha's spine. She released her hold on the trashcan lid and crossed the yard towards the woman sweeping leaves from around the clay pots.

"Did you live here when you were a girl?" she

*The Last Christmas Card*

asked. The woman nodded without looking up.

"This was my Papa's house," she answered. "He used to be a big banker in this city. Bought me my first car as a graduation present. Quite a deal back then, not like it is for every teenager these days." She scattered the leaves towards the bare lawn beyond the stones.

"Did you know the family who used to live here?" asked Samantha. "The Larsens. They lived here during the war." She held her breath as the woman straightened up, one hand resting on her back.

"The Larsens?" she repeated. "Oh, yes, I remember them. They had two children, one was a boy about my age and one was a girl, almost grown when I remember her."

"Was her name Bette?" Samantha's excitement grew, creeping into her voice.

"Bette? Maybe so; we called her Bets when we

*The Last Christmas Card*

were kids." The woman propped her broom against the wall. "Did you know them, too?" she asked.

"No," said Samantha. "But I live in their old house right now and I found something that belonged to Bette–Bets, I mean. I was curious what happened to her."

"She got married after the war, I think. Moved away. So did the rest of the family, when their boy got older. Ben was his name. They had family somewhere outside the city." She moved slowly towards the entrance to her house. "It seems I might have a letter from them somewhere. Wrote to my mama after my papa died."

"May I see it?" asked Samantha, before she realized what she was asking. "I mean, is there any way I can see the address where they moved?"

"Of course, of course," the woman answered. "It's been years since anyone asked about them. A long

*The Last Christmas Card*

time since I even heard their name in this neighborhood. Strange how these things come back again." As she opened the door to the crumbling brownstone's back entrance.

*****

The photograph album was filled with men and women from long ago. Soldiers in uniform, girls in work clothes for the factories, one in a pilot's jacket.

Flora Davies' trembling finger pointed to a photo as Samantha turned the page. "That's Bette Larsen," she said.

A girl in a striped bathing suit, posed on a sandy beach. One hand shaded her face from the glare of the sun as wavy dark hair brushed against her cheeks.

"Taken at the beach the summer I was eight or so," said Ms. Davies. "We were invited to come along for her brother's birthday. My mother took that photo and I remember thinking I wished I would be just as pretty when I grew up."

"Wow," said Samantha, softly. Amazed that Bette Larsen's face was real, that the ghost on the back of the envelope was now flesh and blood.

"You said she was married," Samantha continued. "Do you remember her husband's name? Was he a soldier from Boston?" She held her breath as she waited for the answer.

Ms. Davies frowned. "I remember he worked in a factory somewhere," she answered. "But I don't remember a uniform. But then, I was a little girl with an uncle and cousins in the war, so most of my memories of soldiers are of them."

*The Last Christmas Card*

"So no boys from this neighborhood were soldiers?" she asked, working hard to keep disappointment from showing in her face as the imagined world for Mac Hydberg crumbled away.

"A couple–but this neighborhood didn't have too many older kids at the time. Mostly families with grown boys gone away. Older people, you know."

Samantha's fingers turned the pages, looking at the images of smiling faces, traces of care visible in mothers and boys going off to war. Her hostess's finger tapped another impatiently.

"That's me." A little girl in a sundress, holding a Shirley Temple doll. Part of a woman's skirt was visible, a silky floral pattern.

"How old were you?" asked Samantha. She guessed eight; somewhere there was a photograph of herself at that age, the same spindly legs and knobbly knees beneath a ruffled skirt.

*The Last Christmas Card*

"Eight, I think; or nine." Ms. Davies had risen from the sofa and was rummaging through cubbyholes in a walnut desk. "Somewhere I have it here. Or rather, mama did; she used this desk after my papa died. Kept bills and important notices here, like I did later."

She drew a yellowed scrap of paper from behind a crowd of magazine offers and coupons that easily expired twenty years ago.

"This is it," she said, handing it to Samantha. A tattered envelope with the stamps cut off the corner, an address visible in faint handwriting.

"It's in New York," said Ms. Davies. "I remember now. That's where the Larsens moved; although I don't know about the girl. She went wherever her husband was going, I suppose."

Samantha scribbled the address on a scrap of paper from her pocket. "That's near New Jersey," she muttered to herself, noting the town. "I don't think it's on the coast." Imagining the miles that lay between her and the Larsen family. An address that could easily be a cold trail, given the postmark from 1954.

"Did you ever hear from them again?" she asked, handing the letter to her hostess again. Ms. Davies tucked it out of sight, her face clouding as she considered the question.

"Once—when I was grown, I think—they sent my mama a Christmas card. Could have been '60, maybe earlier. That would've been the last time," she answered.

So maybe even as late as 1960, the Larsens had been in New York. Still over forty years ago, but nothing was impossible.

"What did you find of theirs?" asked Ms. Davies. "Not many leave behind something so important that it matters after all this time."

"Just a letter," Samantha answered. "I thought

*The Last Christmas Card*

maybe someone would want it."

"Well, that's awfully good of you." said Ms. Davies. "Awfully nice." She patted Samantha's hand.

"Would you like to see some other albums?" she asked. "Nothing but photos from when I was a girl, I'm afraid. Old cars and clothes now."

"I would love to," Samantha answered. As Ms. Davies drew something from the book on her lap before closing it.

"Keep this," she said. "I think maybe you should have it. Nobody else will remember it when I'm gone, you know." She rose and carried the book away in quest of another.

Samantha looked down at her hand, the piece of paper resting in her palm. At the smiling face of Bette Larsen in her striped bathing suit.

*The Last Christmas Card*

*****

She pinned Bette Larsen's photo on the fridge, beside the Christmas card. As she surfed the web for phone listings for the name Larsen in Belmont, New York. Then, when the list of possibilities grew depressing, for Bette Hydberg.

It was evening when she dug into a box of takeout, a cup of cocoa brewed from the last in her chocolate canister. Hoping against hope to find an answer somewhere in these listings.

Name after name, number after number. Wrong ages, wrong spelling, wrong family tree.

Apparently, the Larsen family had vanished once again. And Bette Larsen or Hydberg along with them.

*The Last Christmas Card*

\*\*\*\*\*

Samantha strung tinsel across the branches of the pine tree. Strand by strand, the way her mother always had when she was a child. Some of the silver had worn off the pieces, pulled into curls and snarls from previous holidays on an unknown tree for an unknown family.

Nestled in pockets of quilt batting, old dime store ornaments in worn pink and blue. A gold star tarnished with age, a handful of glittered pinecones made out of soft plastic.

Tucked in the attic, they had been forgotten by their previous owner, but they were the closest thing to a traditional Christmas Samantha had known in ages. Her last tree had been a scrubby bush someone stuck

*The Last Christmas Card*

in a pot, jokingly decorating it with painted feathers and chains made from magazine paper.

At the time, it had seemed like the most beautiful tree on earth. Even in the heat of an Australian summer.

She crawled around beneath the folding table, looking for the plug along the baseboard. A strip of wallpaper pulled loose around the plastic cover was the first sign. She shoved the cord into the socket, praying that there were no frayed wires or burnt-out bulbs. Overhead, a flicker of color as the lights burst into bloom. Faded green and gold, white and red, encased in tiny plastic flowers reflecting the colors of the rainbow.

The phone rang beside the sofa. Scurrying out from beneath the table, she reached for the receiver.

"Hello?" she said. Feeling a tingle she couldn't explain before the voice came on the line.

*The Last Christmas Card*

"Are you sitting down?" She recognized Ty's voice on the other end.

"What do you mean?" she asked, confused by his tone and the sound of static on the other end. It must be a cell phone, located somewhere with spotty reception.

"I found Private Mac Hydberg."

She froze for a moment, startled by the words. No reply came to mind at first, as she sank onto the sofa.

"You found him?" she repeated. She heard a short laugh on the other end.

"He's in New York," he said. "Or at least he was. He passed away four years ago at a veteran's hospital near New Jersey. But he has a wife still living."

"Is it Bette?" she leaped ahead of him. "I found someone who knew her and they said she might have gone to New York after the war."

"His spouse is listed as a Bette Hydberg. Resides in an assisted living facility, which is why she doesn't have an address anymore."

"How did you find her?" asked Samantha.

"That's for me to know and you to find out," he answered. "Anyway, I know it's close to Christmas, but ..." He paused for a moment, as if hesitating.

To her surprise, her heart was pounding in her chest as she waited. Almost as if she knew what he was going to say next.

"I have a few days off around Christmas," he said. "If you want, I'll drive you there. You can give Bette her card before Christmas."

Her fingers trembled slightly as she cradled the phone. "All right," she answered. "I'd like that. I wanted you to see how things work out, too." Praying silently that this was some kind of sign; that a miracle awaited in all this for Sergeant Tyler Lars.

"I'll admit I'm curious to see the end of the story," he answered. "I hope it's what you've been wanting, Miss Samantha Sowerman."

"I hope so, too," she answered.

*****

It had taken him three weeks to find the answer. Longer than he'd spent on any other project. In between hours at the office, in between short jogging sessions to try to push his muscles back into strength, he dug up every possible source he could find. Military blogs, World War II history buffs, a series of nonprofit veteran's assistance groups.

Crossing names off the list one by one. Until

*The Last Christmas Card*

he reached Private Mac Hydberg of Belmont, New York.

"I'm sorry, I'm afraid Mr. Hydberg passed away a few years ago," said the nurse at the facility. "Cancer of the liver. He was ill for quite some time."

"Do you know if he had any next of kin?" asked Ty, propping his sore leg on the coffee table as he spoke. "Maybe someone I could speak to about his military years? It's important that I get in touch with them." He pictured a long conversation involving names from Hydberg's unit, dates of battles–but no mention of sweethearts at home or letters written to the states.

"I only know of his wife," answered the nurse. "As far as I know, Mrs. Hydberg is still alive."

"Would you have an address for her?" He clicked his pen, poised over the page. "Maybe a phone number?"

*The Last Christmas Card*

"I'm afraid she doesn't have a direct phone line," answered the nurse.

*Of course, she doesn't...* he thought.

"Or an address on file, either. She and her husband had an apartment at the Belmont Assisted Living facilities. They would have a mailing address for her if you call them. Mrs. Bette Hydberg."

It was too impossible. Too perfect to be true. Even Samantha would have to agree with him on this one.

He paused, before asking "Bette Hydberg, you said?"

"That's correct," the nurse answered.

On Christmas Eve, he was behind the wheel of his car, traveling in the direction of New York's state line. With Samantha in the passenger seat next to him, an old cassette of Christmas classics jammed in his tape player.

*The Last Christmas Card*

Finding her apartment required him to circle the block a few times in the early morning hours, past shabby historic homes in need of repair and brownstones kept in pristine condition by proud homeowners. Until he saw a girl with corkscrew curls and a battered pea green jacket seated on the brick steps of one of the houses.

He pulled into the driveway, noting the frayed knees of her jeans and hem of her t-shirt visible beneath the jacket. Cleary, she was as ill-prepared for cold weather as he was after desert life.

"Thanks for doing this," she said, climbing into the seat. She dropped her shoulder bag onto the floor and pulled a thermos from inside.

"Herbal tea?" she asked. He shook his head.

"No thanks," he answered. "More of a coffee guy, actually." As he pulled away from the frozen curb.

*The Last Christmas Card*

There was mostly silence for the first hour of the drive. The sound of Christmas tunes was the only voice in the car, except when he mumbled an apology for the heating system. One moment blasting like a sauna, the next dead to the touch.

"It's okay, really," she answered. "It's kind of weird to have climate control in cars after so much time in old jeeps and trucks. No heat, no air– sometimes no windows or windshields, either."

"Sounds kind of like some of the vehicles on the road in Iraq," he answered. "Made me appreciate a good military ride, believe me." He drummed his fingers on the steering wheel.

"Look," he cleared his throat, "it'll be a long drive, even leaving this early. So if we have to stop somewhere overnight–" he glanced towards her. "I don't want you to think I'm thinking about asking you to do anything you find wrong. I know what I said about my religion might—"

"I know you're not thinking anything," she answered. "I don't think that just because you have a hard time with your faith means you don't have a moral compass anymore."

He nodded. "Okay. Just so you know." He relaxed slightly, reaching over to play with the stereo knobs.

"Sorry there's not much music selection," he apologized. "No radio reception—my antenna got broken off while the car was parked at a friend's house. That's the problem with being a soldier—needing somebody to baby-sit your things while you're gone. Sometimes they're not exactly like you left them when you get back after a long tour."

"I know the feeling," she answered, with a sympathetic smile. Comfortable at this moment in the knowledge that she really did. She pulled her battered

*The Last Christmas Card*

Bible from inside her bag.

He glanced at it, as if expecting her to launch into a sermon. She could see his jaw tightening, a slightly hunted look as he focused on the highway ahead of them.

"Will you tell me a little bit about what it was like?" she asked. "Your tour of duty, I mean. If you're comfortable with that." She let the book rest on her leg, one hand propped on the cover.

"You're sure about this?" He gave her one of the rare grins she observed before. "It's one of those stories that could go on a long time."

"We've got plenty of time," she answered.

\*\*\*\*\*

*The Last Christmas Card*

"We were sleeping in tents. Sometimes for weeks, a month or two," Ty said. "They'd set one up for a recreation room, but you couldn't get away from the heat and the sand, no matter what. The same old video games and magazines to keep you company when you weren't on duty."

He stirred a spoonful of creamer in his coffee as he sat in a diner booth; across from him, Samantha took a sip from an ice cream float. A girl made equally happy by herbal health teas and soda fountain favorites was something that took him by surprise. Like layers of personality peeling back one by one to the complex core beneath.

"Did you write anybody at home?" she asked. "Friends, maybe? Soldiers stateside?"

"Sometimes," he said. "But a lot of them have families. Lives of their own. They sent care packages, though," he added, after a moment's pause. "You know, a box of prepackaged cookies, a new CD that just came out. Razors and soap."

He took a sip of coffee, pushing aside his finished plate of chicken strips. "You don't think about how much you miss things like that until they're a thousand miles away."

She nodded. "Know what I missed most when I was overseas?" she asked. "Jelly beans. Weird, I know. There's better things–better things for you, too–but I used to love them. Whenever a friend sent me something, they popped a package inside. They'd melt together when I was in Botswana–one giant glob of sugar."

Ty laughed. "Sometimes listening to you talk, I forget that you come from a different experience. Spreading the good word in foreign lands."

She drained the last of the soda from her glass, then bent the straw between her fingers. "Weren't you the one who said there was a lot similar between us?" she asked. "We're just soldiers in different kinds of armies."

"I don't think it's the same," he answered. Pushing up from the table, he moved stiffly to a jukebox in the corner of the diner and studied the selections. Popping a few quarters into the machine, he pushed a button. A moment later, the sound of "White Christmas" drifted from the speakers.

Sliding into his seat again, he offered her a smile. "Classic for soldiers," he said. "Even a white Christmas overseas just isn't the same."

Samantha's chin rested on both her hands as she gazed into his face. "What you meant before," she said. "About them not being the same. Do you mean that?" She searched his face carefully, her eyes meeting his own as if searching their depths.

He sighed. "I don't know," he answered.

"When I was still over there, I talked to God sometimes. When I first went over there, that was all I had. Curse of being a foster kid; no other rocks to cling to except what's inside."

"But why didn't you think of your work as part of His will?" she asked. "You were saving lives; helping people. Without you, others would have died."

"Because the time it mattered most was the one time I couldn't do it," he answered. "When we were caught off-guard that morning. Nobody was looking, it was supposed to be a clean zone. But a second later ..." His voice broke slightly. "A second later, there was nothing anybody could do."

He laughed. "The funny thing is, the only thing that got me through it was faith. There was a chaplain, newly-stationed with my unit. He should've been scared out of his mind, first time seeing that kind of tragedy. But instead, he sat by me the whole time."

*The Last Christmas Card*

Ty reached for his coffee cup, his fingers trembling as they touched the handle. "He propped this postcard next to my bed. The Sermon on the Mount. Said that way I would remember I wasn't alone whenever he couldn't be there." He held the cup in hand, not taking a sip.

"He gave me the card right before they sent me home. A goodbye gift right before I took off. That's the last time I saw him."

After a quiet moment, Samantha spoke. "The last time I saw my mom, she gave me a promise. That I would always have a part of her with me, so long as I kept my faith. And that was the last thing she ever gave me."

Reaching across, she touched his hand. "Your faith is like Private Hydberg's card. It just got lost between the past and where you are now."

"You think it's just gonna show up someday,

like the card in your mailbox?" he asked.

Her eyes met his with a gentle gleam. "The card needed some help to get to its destination, remember?" she asked.

He didn't move his fingers away from the warmth of her touch. Instead, he let them intertwine with hers, in a sudden gesture that sent her heartbeat skipping wildly.

"You make me think about how long I've been away from that part of my life," he said, softly. "Maybe it's the missionary part, I don't know. Maybe it's the way you stuck with this card all the way to a diner two states away." He ran his hand over his face, trying to hide the smile creeping across his features.

"How do you know you weren't already looking for signs?" she replied, softly.

Instead of answering, he leaned forward and cupped her face, drawing her closer. His lips touched

*The Last Christmas Card*

hers, brushing softly before the kiss.

It took her by surprise, but so did the realization that she had wanted this for a long time. Her hand reached up to cradle his wrist, trace his hand against her face.

He drew back after a moment. "Was that okay?" he whispered. "I didn't intend–but I've been wishing for that for awhile." He sounded boyish, almost apologetic as his eyes met hers.

Samantha's fingers brushed against his hair. "I have too," she said, with a faint laugh. "I guess I just didn't know it until now."

The jukebox song switched to the slow, familiar sounds of "The Christmas Song" as someone inserted new quarters into the slot. A cool breeze swept over them as the door jangled open, sending a shiver through the patrons.

Ty stirred, glancing out the window where the

first snow flurries appeared. "We should go," he murmured. "We don't want to get snowed in here when we're so close." Gently, he drew his fingers from hers.

"No, we don't." Samantha pulled a few bills from her pocket and laid them on the table. Her hand still tingled with warmth, a sudden blush causing her to lower her eyes from Ty's.

The snow grew heavier a few miles from the diner, thick drifts along the ditch and coating the highway. Ty's car poked along the road, the windshield wipers working furiously against the white flakes.

Peering through the windshield, Ty scowled. "We should've left sooner," he said. "If we get stuck somewhere–" He didn't finish, glancing at her before turning back to the road.

"It's okay," she said. "I always carry a couple

*The Last Christmas Card*

of pocket-sized thermal blankets in my bag. Just in case."

He gave her an incredulous look. "Are you serious?" he said.

She shrugged. "I may be in the states, but my mind is still other places. And I never remember to take anything out of my pockets once it's inside."

It was the first time she heard him laugh like that. Without a trace of bitterness or sadness.

\*\*\*\*\*

Ty nosed the car into a spot in the Belmont Assisted Living parking lot, its lines invisible through the blanket of snow over the pavement. A dusting of flakes began covering the windshield a moment after

*The Last Christmas Card*

he shut off the wipers.

"Well, shall we?" he asked.

Samantha shouldered her bag. "I guess so," she answered. A trace of nervousness in her voice as she opened the car door. Ahead was the building's main office, surrounded by box shrubs transformed into white orbs by the snow.

The main hall was heated, an area rug just inside to protect the main carpeting from snow flurries. A row of apartment mail boxes beside a potted banana tree, a row of doors ahead in the corridor. Samantha checked the names and numbers against the slip of paper in her hand. Mrs. Bette Hydberg, Apartment 132.

"She must be down another hallway," Ty said, glancing at the doors as they passed. "There aren't enough doors–take a left up here." He pointed towards the end of the hall, where it branched off in two directions. One a short passage to vending machines and laundry services, the other, a second hall of apartments. Including door 132.

Samantha raised her hand to knock, the pressure pushing the door partly open. Unlatched, the crack revealing a messy stack of books and household linens.

"Hello?" she called. "Mrs. Hydberg?" She pushed it open all the way, half-fearing the resident was in distress. An echo of silence in the room. Behind her, Ty leaned against the door.

"Maybe she went out for a few minutes," he suggested.

"Excuse me, are you looking for somebody?" A voice behind them spoke up. They turned to see a nurse carrying an armful of collapsed cardboard boxes, the name "Cindy" stamped on her name tag.

"For Mrs. Hydberg," said Samantha. "Is this

her apartment?" She pointed towards the open door.

"It was," the nurse answered, brushing past her as she made her way inside. "Mrs. Hydberg's been transferred out of here, I'm afraid. Couple of days ago."

"Do you know where they transferred her?" asked Ty.

"Over to the nursing home," answered Cindy. "It's across town. She's pretty bad now. Gets confused easily, doesn't take her meds or eat her meals. She couldn't be left alone any longer and since she doesn't have any family ..."

"No family?" repeated Samantha. "No kids?" The nurse shook her head.

"She and her husband couldn't have any, apparently." She glanced from Samantha to Ty. "Are you two related to the Hydberg's somehow?"

"Just some concerned friends," Ty answered.

*The Last Christmas Card*

"Miss Sowerman here found some personal papers that belong to Mrs. Hydberg and wanted to return them."

Cindy nodded. "Well, it's kind of ironic, since what I'm doing right now is boxing up her personal stuff." She pointed towards the jumble of personal possessions, books and knickknacks. "I figure we'll track down another branch of her family and send them there. Maybe a cousin or a great-niece or nephew or something. Mrs. Hydberg never left instructions about what to do with her things if she became too ill to look after her apartment."

"It seems so sad," said Samantha, lifting up an old schoolbook and paging through it. "That there's nobody left to care after all these years." Cindy placed a few old records in the box, a clay sculpture obviously molded by a child.

"Oh, they had quite a love story, apparently," the nurse answered. "They were crazy about each other, never spent a night apart. When he died, her health just went downhill." She placed a stack of old scrapbooks and framed photos inside.

Samantha lifted the cover of one of the books, revealing a series of brightly colored snapshots from the fifties. Bette Larsen all grown up in a silk dress, an older couple at a picnic table.

A few pages back, wartime photos in black and white. A solemn-looking boy in a soldier's uniform, posed in front of a brownstone entrance. Mac Hydberg?

She touched the photo, glancing below at a water-stained image of two people. The color photo of Bette in yellow chiffon, the young man now in a grey suit, his arm around her shoulder.

"Ty, look," she said. "It's Mac Hydberg." He moved closer, leaning over to study the photograph.

"You knew him?" asked the nurse.

"No," answered Samantha. "I just wanted to know what he looked like." She pulled the photo of Bette from her pocket.

"Somebody gave me this. A friend," she added. "Of Mrs. Hydberg when she was younger. She said since I was trying to return Bette's letter, I should at least see what she looked like back then."

Cindy laughed. "That's her, all right," she answered. "Mr. Hydberg kept one like that in his wallet. He called her Bets and made everybody call him Mac."

"Did you ever meet him?" asked Ty, looking up from the photograph album.

Cindy nodded. "I knew him pretty well. He was a good man, a strong believer," she answered. "He bought Mrs. Hydberg flowers every week. Used to whittle prizes for the facility fundraiser." She assembled a second cardboard box. "Somewhere

*The Last Christmas Card*

around here, she has his war uniform. I guess since they didn't have a son or grandson, there was no one to give it to."

Samantha closed the book and placed it in the box. "Can you tell us how to get to the nursing home?" she asked. "I'd really like to see her, if I can."

"Sure." Cindy paused in her packing, rummaging around on a nearby table. She pulled a pad and pencil from beneath a pile of newspaper.

"This is the shortest route across town. The nursing home's on this side street, not far from the school." Her pencil sketched out lines and numbers quickly. "Just watch out for traffic–it's almost five o' clock and Christmas Eve, so the road will be pretty packed with cars. Plus, the snow makes it all slower." She tore off the piece of paper and handed it to Ty.

"Bette doesn't have many visitors," said Cindy. "If they'll let you stop by, then it'll be a real treat for

*The Last Christmas Card*

her. She must be pretty lonely there; just memories for company."

Ty reached into his wallet and drew out one of his business cards. "If anything should happen to Mrs. Hydberg, then you can contact us at this number," he said. "We'd like to know if she's okay or if she needs something." The nurse glanced at it.

"You're with the military?" she said. "From Connecticut?"

Ty smiled faintly. "Yes, Ma'am," he answered. "Miss Sowerman here is a missionary from Massachusetts."

She shook her head as she slipped the card into her smock pocket. "I can't get over you two coming all this way," she said. "Just to bring somebody a lost item."

Reaching down, she flipped open the book and pulled something out. "Wait a second," she said, stopping them in the doorway. "I think you should have this."

She handed it to Ty, who was closest. The photo of Mac Hydberg from the album, posed in his military uniform.

"Bette would have wanted it that way," she said. "Something to remember Mac by, since she's the last family he has. Now you've got a matching one to go with Bette's there."

"Thank you," said Ty. He slipped the photo in his pocket and followed Samantha into the hall. Glancing back to see Cindy watching from the doorway with a goodbye wave.

*****

*The Last Christmas Card*

Cindy wasn't lying about the traffic. In a snarl of cars and buses downtown, Samantha and Ty watched the lines of vehicles crawl along through traffic lights and constant snowfall. A tinsel Christmas tree swung from the lamppost in a gust of wind. Red metallic balls glinting in the flash of lights from a wrecker a few feet ahead of them.

"We'll never make it by visiting hours," said Samantha. "It's the holidays, so they probably sent as many people home early as possible."

"Maybe they'll bend the rules," Ty answered. "It's Christmas Eve, you know. There will be family stopping by, probably."

"She doesn't have any family," Samantha reminded him. "I guess the Larsens must have moved away. Or maybe her brother didn't have any children, either."

"Sad," Ty said. "To think that there's nobody

*The Last Christmas Card*

left." His expression clouding with gloom as he flicked the right turn signal.

The parking lot for the nursing home was large and empty, the yard lights blazing like beacons beneath their snowy caps. In the grey light, Ty climbed from the driver's seat, waiting as Samantha emerged. He could see the card in her hand, held tightly for its final journey.

"Watch your step," he said. "There's a few patches of ice under this snow." He held out his arm in a gentlemanly gesture. After a short pause, she took hold of it.

"Just don't let me pull you down," she teased.

In the foyer of the nursing home, a small Christmas tree winked with clear lights and matching silver and gold ornaments. Behind the desk, an aide glanced over a pile of reports as a Christmas choir hummed from her computer's speakers.

*The Last Christmas Card*

"Excuse me," Samantha approached, leaning over the counter. "We're here to see Bette Hydberg. We were told she was a patient here."

The aide lowered her file. "Are you family of Bette's?" she asked.

"No," Samantha answered. "Just friends."

"There are no names on Bette's visitor's list," said the aide. "You may not have been informed that this is a closed facility. Patients only receive pre-approved visitors they place on their lists, usually family."

"It's important," pleaded Samantha. "It's Christmas Eve. If we could just see her for a few minutes–"

"That would be against the rules," the nurse answered. "I'm sorry." She gave Samantha a sympathetic smile.

Disappointment and frustration washed over

*The Last Christmas Card*

Samantha's face, the first trace of tears gathering in her eyes. She took a deep breath as she held up the envelope.

"Then could you–" She felt Ty's hand on her arm, gently moving her aside.

"Excuse me, Ma'am, I'm from Veteran's Affairs," he said. "And I'm here with regards to Mrs. Hydberg's late husband, Private Mac Hydberg." He pulled out his wallet, flipping it open to his I.D. card.

"If we could just have a few minutes of Mrs. Hydberg's time, I would appreciate it," he said.

The aide studied the I.D. card carefully, then nodded. "If you're from Veteran's Affairs, I suppose I can make an exception."

She glanced at the clock. "It's almost six-thirty. The residents are being wheeled to the recreation room around seven for a special Christmas Eve concert, so you have until then. The room is 227, just down the hall." She pushed a button beneath the desk, buzzing open the door to the main hall.

"Thank you," Ty answered, taking Samantha's arm and steering her through the doors.

"Don't look back," he whispered, "I don't want her to change her mind."

"Thanks for doing that," she said, keeping her voice low. "I thought it was over and we were so close." Her fingers were clamped tightly around the envelope. Her palm was sweating as she took Ty's hand for a moment, his skin cool and damp to the touch.

The rooms slipped by as they walked. One by one, until the number 227 was visible.

*****

*The Last Christmas Card*

Samantha pushed the half-ajar door open and slipped inside. The lighting was dim, a small touch lamp glowing on a table. A woman sat dozing in an armchair, a holly-patterned bathrobe drawn around her.

"Mrs. Hydberg?" Samantha approached. "I'm sorry to interrupt–"

The woman's eyes flickered open. "Is it you, Lissy?" she asked. "Never mind about that cake now. I'm too tired to make one for supper." She stirred, her fingers feeling around for a cane leaning against the chair's arm.

"My name is Samantha," said Sam, reaching to touch the woman's hand as she sat down across from her. "I came to bring you a Christmas card. From Mac."

For a moment, Bette Hydberg's face cleared.

*The Last Christmas Card*

"Mac," she whispered. "Why yes, I know him. Such a fine boy. From a good family." Her hand fumbled, reached over to pat Samantha's.

"We're sweethearts, you know," she whispered. "Of course, we haven't told anybody yet. We're both too young, they say."

"He mailed you a card from overseas," said Samantha. "But it never arrived. Did he tell you about it?" She held out the envelope, the address facing Bette.

Bette took hold of it, confusion on her face. "He wouldn't write to me sometimes," she said. "In the war, I mean. He got upset about something; thought I had another boyfriend, I suppose. It was such a long time before he would write me letters again." She sighed, her hand trembling in Samantha's.

"Do you want me to read it to you?" asked Samantha. "Mac's card? It's been waiting for you for over sixty years." Turning it over, she lifted the flap where it had resealed itself after closing.

Bette's eyes widened as Samantha drew the card from inside. The blue and white scene of the village, the star blazing above.

"Dear Bets," she read aloud. "I hope you're reading this somewhere alone before Christmas and that you're having a swell time. I'll bet you've been too busy to write many letters with all that studying for exams. I hope you do the best in your class. Your mama will be proud of you and you'll be a graduate by the time I get back from this war."

"My exams," said Bette. "Oh, I used to study and study. I remember once..." she trailed off, before adding, "...once he coached me through geography. Showing me all those countries in Europe. I never thought he would go to one, though."

"He says he carries your photo everywhere he

*The Last Christmas Card*

goes," said Samantha. "Here he says, 'I guess I think about you all the time, even when it seems like home is a million miles away and I'll never get back there. It must be Christmas that makes it feel this way'..." As she read, she watched Bette's face change, her grey eyes swimming with tears as she listened.

"Do you think about me?" Samantha paused at this line, afraid of going on. The words were causing Bette more pain than happiness as she gazed at the faded card in Samantha's hand.

Bette's voice trembled. "I think about him all the time," she said. "Oh, every day. I wish he would come back from that terrible war." Her voice choked.

Samantha's fingers creased the edge of the card, her mind trying to find the right words for the woman lost in her memories. A noise in the doorway made Samantha turn towards the sound. Ty had slipped inside the room. He crouched down beside

*The Last Christmas Card*

Bette's chair and touched her hand.

"Hello, Bette," he said. She raised her head from her lap, her face lighting up at the sound of Ty's voice.

In the dark, his face was hard to see, a silhouette of a man's figure. The light caught the faded military insignia on his jacket. Bette's fingers reached eagerly to touch it, recognizing the Army symbol.

"Mac?" she said. "It's you, isn't it?" A flutter of hope in her voice, like a frail bird beating against a cage's wire bars. Her fingers closed around his hand, clutching it tightly.

"This girl brought me your Christmas card," she said. "All the way from the war. Do you remember?" she asked him. "She was reading it to me. You wrote it, didn't you?"

"Of course I did," he answered. "The Christmas in Belgium. I remember." He squeezed her fingers gently.

"Do you want me to finish it for you?" he asked. Reaching over, he pulled the card from Samantha's hand. Scanning the lines briefly before he spoke.

"If there's a chance you'll feel the same when the war's over, then tell me so. Tell me you'll keep waiting until I make it back. That way I'll have something to hold onto." He paused for a moment, his voice thickening. "Merry Christmas, Bets. Love, Mac."

Carefully, he refolded the card and laid it on Bette's lap. She held onto his hand, her lips moving as they formed a smile.

"I do, Mac," she whispered. "I think about you every day. I always remember. I waited so long for you to write and when you didn't, I knew how I really felt." A tear rolled down her face.

*The Last Christmas Card*

"It's all right," he answered, soothingly. "There will be more letters, I promise. But I wanted you to have this card in time for Christmas. To know I was thinking of you the whole time."

"I missed you so much. I've been waiting so long for you to come back," she said. "You promise everything is all right?"

He held her hand in both of his now, a soft smile as he replied. "I know," he said. "I know you waited, Bets."

"We were happy, weren't we," she whispered. "We were happy together. You and I."

"Of course we were," he said. Reaching up, he touched her cheek. The tear was followed by another; Bette smiled into his face as her trembling fingers reached to touch his hand."

"Merry Christmas, Bets," he whispered.

Her eyes drooped closed. One hand resting on

the card, drawing it closer.

"Merry Christmas, Mac," she murmured. Leaning forward, he kissed her on the forehead, then rose to leave. Placing the card's envelope on her lap, next to the blue and white village from sixty years ago.

*****

Samantha waited in the hallway as Ty closed the door behind them.

"That was incredible," she said. "What you did for her ... I can't thank you enough for that." She wiped her eyes, feeling the trace of tears on her fingers.

He shook his head. "No thanks necessary. It was just a Christmas present for a friend."

She could see the tenderness beneath the

surface of his gaze. Reaching for his cheek, she gently traced his jawline.

"You're really something, Sergeant Lars," she said. Warmth spilling into the depths of her brown eyes as she locked her gaze with his.

"This from the girl who traveled hundreds of miles to deliver a Christmas card," he answered, softly, a hint of sadness creeping into his voice. The faint flicker of a smile visible momentarily before vanishing again.

"That card may have made Bette's Christmas," he whispered. "I guess you were right after all. About it mattering."

She let out a laugh. "It wouldn't have mattered if you hadn't helped me," she answered. "Thank you. I mean for everything."

Shrugging his shoulders, he zipped up his coat. "We should go now. Before the storm picks up again," he said, nodding towards the door.

He placed his hand on her shoulder, guiding her towards the main entrance. They passed a handful of residents being wheeled towards the recreation room by aides, where a Christmas tree glittered near an unlit fireplace. A row of high school students in choir robes, a young woman with her ear bent towards an Irish harp as she plucked its strings.

Outside, the snow coated the hood of the car, inches deep as they trudged towards the parking lot. Samantha glanced up into the sky, where heavy white flakes were falling in a fast, thick cloud.

Behind those clouds, stars were twinkling like the silver one on the card. That was her thought as she slid her arm through Ty's, feeling the gentle pressure of his hand as it wrapped around hers.

*The Last Christmas Card*

\*\*\*\*\*

In the car, Samantha sipped the remains of her thermos of tea. Lukewarm from hours of sitting in the cold car. She glanced at Ty, whose fingers were toying with the knob to the car's heating system. A rasping sound from the vents as it blew a draft of cool air on both of them.

"I've been thinking about what you said, Ty," she said, screwing the lid on her thermos again. "About these last few weeks bringing you closer to your faith."

He snorted. "I don't know if I would go that far," he answered. "I said it made me remember those times."

"You said it made you miss them," she argued. "I think that's a pretty big deal. For someone who

claims he doesn't have a rock to cling to anymore."
She held out the thermos, but he shook his head.

"What I feel ..." he hesitated. "What I feel for you is ... is something we should be careful about."

His voice was rough, emotion buried in its tones. She stared at him, feeling confused.

"What do you mean, careful?" she asked. "Ty, when I talked about our confession, I wasn't trying to pressure you into a relationship with me."

"With you, no," he said. "With God, yes." He looked away from the road to meet her eyes.

"Half of this has been about you, Sam," he said. "I could pretend that wanting to live by faith is the point, but right at this moment, it's not. What I did today, I did for you. Plain and simple."

He caught a glint of accusation in her eyes before he looked away again, the windshield wipers sweeping a path of vision to the road ahead. He seemed grateful for the distraction, making her cheeks scarlet with frustration.

"How can you say it's all about me?" she asked. "I saw you with Bette; at that moment, your focus was on her, not me. When you had no clue that I would show up at the Hydberg house, you went there alone to learn the truth from them. If you wanted to impress me there were easier ways. I think you were trying to accomplish something else." Reaching over, she closed the shutters to the vent's cool stream.

"What?" he asked. "Impressing God? Somehow I think He wants something more than a road trip to Pennsylvania over a Christmas card."

"I think all He wants is for you to believe in Him again," she answered.

A rasping sound emerged from the heat vents as Ty's hand smacked the dash. A sputter, followed by a rushing wave of heat.

*The Last Christmas Card*

"So everything we talked about at the restaurant," he said. "That was just for the sake of my walk with God. None of it was us. About what you feel for me." A cold edge crept into his voice.

"That's not what I said," she answered. "That's what you're making it out to be. Because you're not willing to admit your soul is more important.

A hollow laugh emerged from his throat. "Yeah, I guess that's the most important part if you're a missionary, isn't it?" He gripped the steering wheel, fingers white against the dark vinyl. "I should've remembered that when we were in the restaurant today."

Biting her lip, Samantha stared at the window, unwilling to respond. His coldness cut through her like a knife after what happened today. From the kiss in the diner to the sound of him reading Mac's words to Bette–this shouldn't be the way those moments ended.

*The Last Christmas Card*

A fight over whether Ty's eternal salvation outweighed the brief connection between two hearts.

The cassette tape had fallen silent, ejected from the player. The sound of passing traffic and radio static filled the rest of the ride. By the time they reached Boston, the pink light of dawn appeared on the horizon. Ty circled around the block, pulling into an empty space in front of Samantha's house.

He shifted the car into park, the motor running. Silently, she gathered her bag and thermos, her fingers closing around the door handle.

"Thanks for driving me there," she said.

"No problem," he answered. His eyes flickering towards her briefly, his smile forced.

She shrugged. "I'll see you around sometime, maybe." She climbed out, closing the door behind her. Aware that his eyes were focused on her for a long moment as she fumbled through her pocket for her

*The Last Christmas Card*

house keys. Waiting for her to climb the steps before he shifted into reverse and pulled onto the street again. His car drove towards the end of the block, the veteran's insignia on his license plate barely visible to her gaze as he signaled a left turn up ahead.

"Merry Christmas, Sergeant Lars," she whispered. Then climbed the steps to the cold rooms and unlit tree awaiting her inside for the holidays.

\*\*\*\*\*

Two days after Christmas, the application for the Brazilian medical missions program arrived by email. Samantha printed off the pages, sorting through the blanks and questionnaires that would bend her life path in a new direction.

*The Last Christmas Card*

Her mind was elsewhere, however; still thinking of a Christmas card from sixty years before. And the sound of Ty's voice reading the last few lines to a woman whose memories dwelled on a soldier's blue Christmas overseas.

She had phoned Ty's office the day after Christmas. The phone rang without answer; the second time she called, a voice came on the line to inform her that he was on vacation. She left messages, none of which were returned.

Had she pushed him too hard? Her mind replayed their moments together, the rare glimpse of a genuine smile when he let his guard down. He had seemed so close to finding peace again, but his conversation in the car snatched back the words from the diner.

He had accused her of treating him like a mission project, as if her heart had never felt anything for him but the concern of a fellow Christian. The memory of his words stung whenever they drifted into her thoughts. She stirred her cup of tea, wishing she could forget the bitter part and remember the sweetness alone. But life's flavors were mingled between the two, a divine reminder that this existence was a brief window of opportunity for the heart and soul.

Failing to convince Ty of that truth hurt worst of all.

Her pencil scribbled answers into the blanks, about her experience in languages, her life in faraway villages. It always helped her to write out the answers before she typed them, giving her a chance to think about each one. A trick her mother used for job applications, she remembered.

In the "next of kin" blank she wrote "none". There was no one they should call if there was an emergency. The pain of knowing that no human heart would be hurt by her loss was comforted in the knowledge that her work was meant for the One who cared the most.

The realization startled her, that only a few days ago she had entertained feelings that someone like Ty would want to know if something happened to her. Would care deeply, perhaps, if she was lost–all while understanding the risk was worth the mission. After all, there were more connections between a missionary and a soldier than met the eye.

She wondered if there had been anyone to care if Ty had been lost. Or if his name would have mattered only as an entry on a list of casualties of war.

The photograph of Bette Larsen was still clipped to her fridge, alongside the young Mac Hydberg in uniform. Ty had slipped it into her bag after they left the nursing home, apparently. She found

*The Last Christmas Card*

it there when she arrived home, its edge sticking out slightly between the pages of her Bible. His way of a offering her a Christmas present, maybe. Or a goodbye kinder than the one between them in the car.

Maybe she would try to phone him again. Maybe this time he would finally answer.

\*\*\*\*\*

The red light on Ty's answering machine flashed repeatedly, but he didn't push the button. He let the messages pile up as he flipped through the television channels, his leg propped on the coffee table.

He hadn't felt like a jog, recently. His aspirin bottle was almost empty, but he hadn't bothered to replace it in the cabinet. Limping from room to room, an occasional trip to the front lawn to collect the paper. As if his interest in life had begun slipping away by inches, leaving him listless again.

"So when are you coming back to work?" One of his coworkers phoned one evening to ask about a recent report. "You taking a couple of weeks off?"

"I don't know," Ty answered. "Just needed some personal time, that's all." He scrolled through an internet site on careers, trying to muster enthusiasm for the list of retail security posts and sales positions.

"A girl called for you. A couple of times, actually. She left a message, her name's Samantha Sowerman–"

"Yeah, I know," he answered. "I'm on it." Actually, he was tempted to delete them without listening, to avoid hearing her voice again. Reminding him of that last conversation in the car, when he blew off the opportunity to make their connection into a future.

If a future was possible for him, that is. He was restless, in need of a change, but with no idea where to start. Was it his job? His attitude? Being stuck between the life of a soldier and the life of a civilian gave him no place to start. Maybe that's why Samantha kept pushing him to open up to God. A rock would be a starting point; a home base to stand in search of a future path.

Maybe she was the answer. And instead of accepting her help, he pushed her away.

He closed his laptop and pressed his face in his hands. It had been a long time since he prayed, but the urge to speak to God was stronger at this moment than any he had known since he left Iraq.

The chaplain's final words to him: *God wants to talk to you, Ty. Speak up more often so He doesn't*

*The Last Christmas Card*

*have to shout to get your attention.*

"What do you want me to do?" Ty murmured. "Tell me what's supposed to happen, Lord. 'Cause I don't have a clue what comes next." That was all that emerged from his lips, followed by the silence of an empty house.

No answer, no sign. Nothing but the flicker of static on the muted television screen. As he stretched out on the sofa, he wondered what the missionary girl would say about that. Probably that he wasn't trying hard enough. Or being open enough.

Whatever. He flipped the station to a late-night movie and let his eyes sink closed beneath the wash of grainy color and shadow.

\*\*\*\*\*

*The Last Christmas Card*

*Rap, rap, rap.* The sound of faint knocking interrupted Ty's dream. He opened his eyes, blinking to adjust to the harsh light pouring in the window. Two-fifteen. Whoever was at the door had roused him from sleeping through the day.

He had a fleeting thought that someone had given Samantha his address. A strange tingle passed through his body, vanishing with the thought of someone from the office dropping by to check up on him.

Pushing aside the classified section of the paper, he straightened his shirt and moved towards the door. Shifting his weight from his stiffened leg as he pulled it open. On the other side was a woman who looked vaguely familiar, wearing a flowered blouse and jeans.

"Sergeant Lars?" she asked.

*The Last Christmas Card*

He nodded. "Yes, Ma'am," he answered. Trying to suppress a frown as he struggled to place her face.

"It's Cindy from Belmont Assisted Living," she said. "You gave me your card–"

"Of course," he answered. No wonder she looked familiar. "Please, come inside." He opened the door, motioning towards the sofa inside.

"I can't stay long," she said. "But you said to let you know if anything happened to Mrs. Hydberg. She passed away a couple days after Christmas. I thought you should know, since you and your friend were so interested in her."

"I'm sorry," he answered. His mind reeling at the surprise of the statement, thinking of how to tell Samantha. She would probably be hurt by the news after spending so much time absorbed with Bette Hydberg's story.

*The Last Christmas Card*

Cindy reached down and lifted a box from the steps. "I brought you some of her things," she said. "I know it seems strange, but none of the relatives we contacted wanted them. There was no one else who cared about her story but you two. So I boxed up the things that meant the most to Bette."

She placed it on the coffee table. "Bette would be glad to know that somebody was still interested in her life. So I think she would want you to have these things."

Shocked, he raised his eyebrows. "You're giving me her things?" he said, looking at the box on his table. A few days ago, he held the hand of the woman whose life it held. He had looked through her photographs, even read the words her husband had written over sixty years ago. Now her most treasured earthly possessions were in his keeping.

Cindy nodded. "If you're interested," she said.

"But I thought you would be, after you dropped by on Christmas Eve. I have a family event a few miles from here, so I looked up your address online and brought the box with me."

He lifted the top, spotting photo albums tucked inside, the framed pictures of Bette and Mac, the scrapbooks containing their mementos. A folded layer of army green fabric: Private Mac Hydberg's uniform. He touched the sleeve, imagining the soldier who wore it. The solemn face in that photograph Cindy gave them, of a young man risking everything for his country, including the possibility of losing a future with the girl he loved.

"I don't know what to say," he said. "I mean, I'm amazed you would take this kind of time for someone."

She shrugged. "You did. Bringing a letter to a total stranger like that." She turned towards the door, then paused.

"One more thing." She reached into her pocket and drew an envelope from it.

"The letter you brought to Bette on Christmas Eve," she said. Placing the envelope on top of the box.

He opened the door for her, stepping onto the porch with a slight limp that he hoped she didn't notice. "Thank you again for dropping this off. Sam– Miss Sowerman will be really grateful you took the time for Bette."

"Tell her I said hello," said Cindy. As she unlocked her car door, she gave him a friendly smile. "You two make a cute couple." Giving him a knowing smile before closing the door.

He waved goodbye, feeling as if he was trapped in a dream. A surreal awakening, the end of the story that made the last few weeks so vivid and alive. The closest thing to a mission he had known

*The Last Christmas Card*

since his return to the U.S.

Would the missionary girl call this a sign? A box of reminders showing up on his doorstep, connecting him in every way to the experience he shared with her. Things which Bette Hydberg let go of even as she clung to the memories of her long-ago love.

He closed his eyes. *Lord, show me what comes next. Show me the future you want me to have. Teach me to trust you again, because I don't know what to do next.*

*****

Samantha's mother always allowed her to stay up until midnight on New Year's Eve. Sometimes they wore paper hats, playing Chinese checkers and watching the television until the ball dropped in Times Square.

Some people had fireworks, some had glasses of champagne. Samantha and her mother had paper whistles to blow at the stroke of midnight.

She was thinking of this as she packed the Christmas ornaments in their padded box again. New Year's morning and she was cross-legged on the floor, packing up someone else's ornaments for their trip back to the attic. Where she supposed they would remain until Mrs. Lindell cleaned out the space or the new renters grew curious about what was upstairs.

They would probably still be there when she was in Brazil, translating the Christmas story into local dialect for children at the medical mission. A holiday spent with a hand-molded clay creche, a tree decorated with paper chains and flowers. A spicy bowl of rice

*The Last Christmas Card*

with chicken for Christmas dinner.

Stripping the tinsel from the branches, she slipped it into the crumbling box again, beside scattered Christmas cards from years ago. The sight of them made her think of Bette Hydberg. And something else, although she couldn't admit to Ty's memory without a pang. He had never returned her calls, even after a week of waiting.

She had taken a crock of soup to Flora Davies' house a few days before, spending some time with the neighbor who helped her find the answer.

"And so they got married," said Flora. "I'm glad to hear it. So many boys didn't come back. Others came back to not much, you know."

"I know," answered Samantha. With a slight pain as she thought of Tyler Lars returning to a desk job and an empty life.

"But what about you? You'll be all alone when

*The Last Christmas Card*

you go to South America, won't you?" said Flora, remembering Samantha's upcoming trip. "But I suppose you're used to that, aren't you? As a missionary." Her face brightened. "But then you'll have your fellow missionaries. Sort of a band of brothers in Christ." She patted Samantha's arm.

Another parallel with the life of a soldier. As Samantha forced herself to smile in reply.

She placed the lid on the box of Christmas balls and stacked it with the others by the stairs. As she straightened up, the door's buzzer sounded.

The mail was due; probably a package delivered, a late present from one of the relatives who remembered her around this time. She opened the door, expecting to see the blue jacket of a postal worker.

Instead, she saw a faded coat with a military insignia on the sleeve. The arm wrapped around a big cardboard box.

"Ty?" she said. Staring at a pair of blue eyes peering above the folded cardboard flaps.

"Can I come in?" he asked. As the door opened wider, he crossed the threshold, glancing around at the worn entryway, its lamps dim from low-watt and missing bulbs.

"Um, your apartment," he began. She gestured towards the open door to the old dining room.

"This way," she said. "It's um, kind of messy I'm afraid." A shower of pine needles visible beneath the tree on the table, a torn piece of wrapping paper from a Christmas present from her landlady.

He placed the box on her coffee table. Stuffing his hands into his pockets as he turned towards her.

"Sam," he began. "Bette Hydberg passed away. A couple of days after we met her."

A look of shock crossed her face. "Dead?" she

said. "Then we–then I guess we were just in time." Her mouth trembled slightly as she glanced towards the photo on the fridge.

Crossing her arms, she met his eyes. "So why did you drive here to tell me?" she asked. "You could have phoned. I left you messages." Her gaze traveled towards the box.

"Those are her things," he said. "Cindy–from the nursing home–brought me this box a couple of days ago. Bette's photos and things."

As she opened the lid, he added, "I wanted you to have them."

She stared at the objects inside, touching the photograph album on top, the same one she opened when they were in Bette's room in the nursing home. For the first time, tears gathered in her eyes.

"These are her and Mac's possessions," she said. "Their whole lives are here. But why–" She

*The Last Christmas Card*

glanced over her shoulder at Ty, confused.

He shrugged. "I was the only person Cindy could think of who would want them. They would've ended up in a donation box somewhere otherwise."

He stepped closer, closing the distance between them. "I'm glad she did. Because if she hadn't, I never would've come back here to apologize to you. To tell you that you were right. About me, about my feelings ..."

"You mean about us," she said, looking away, not daring to hope that it was anything else. Her voice choked with emotion as he grew closer. Her palms pressed into her arms, fingers trembling.

"I mean about my faith," he said. "I asked Him for a sign, something to make me move on with my life instead of ending up stuck between two lives. And He sent you, but I was just too blind to see it."

Reaching for her face, he touched her cheek.

*The Last Christmas Card*

"So I guess He had to wait until I was ready. Only this time, He sent it to me in a box of stuff instead."

She couldn't speak; her heart was pounding, knowing what he would say next.

"If I'm ready to change," he whispered, "will you help me, Sam? Whatever it takes, I want to follow that path with Him again."

Her fingers touched his hand, taking it in her own. "You know I will," she said. Her eyes meeting his with a gaze as intense as his own. "I've wanted to from the moment we met. You knew that."

"No matter what it takes," he said. His voice shifted to a teasing whisper as he added, "even if I find myself in Brazil, helping roll bandages in a mission hospital."

"Do you think that's God's plan for you?" she retorted, half-teasing, half-curious.

His face grew serious for a moment. "Maybe.

*The Last Christmas Card*

Since I think He wants me to start over with you."

Leaning down, he pressed his lips against hers, cradling her face. She kissed him back, her arms wrapping around his shoulders tightly.

A long moment passed before he drew back, giving her one of those rare open smiles. The kind of smile she had wanted to see on his face since that day they met in the cafe.

"One more thing," he said. Reaching into his pocket, he pulled out a small package, wrapped in Christmas paper. Slipping it into her hand, watching with a smile as her fingers tugged at the string.

Inside was a familiar envelope, the spidery veins of black ink in Mac Hydberg's handwriting. A glimpse of blue and white visible beneath the open flap.

"The card," said Samantha. "She brought you the card, too?"

*The Last Christmas Card*

He nodded. "She said that Bette would want us to have it," he said. "But I think she was really thinking of you. The girl who would travel all those miles to deliver a Christmas card mailed to her house."

She touched the fragile paper with her fingertip. "I guess it's home now," she said. Her smile growing sad for a moment as she spoke. "Part of Bette and Mac's story, like the photos in the box."

Ty slid his arm around her shoulders. "We'll find a place to keep them safe," he said. "Some place where you can store them until you're ready to give them a home."

"All except this," she answered. "This one stays–no matter where we end up." She held up the envelope in her hand. "After all, it's what got us here, right?"

"No," he corrected her, ruffling her curls softly. "That would be God, remember?"

*The Last Christmas Card*

"I remember," she answered. Her hand slipping inside his, fingers intertwined as she leaned against him.

Gently, her other hand slid the envelope between the pages of her cracked leather Bible. Where it lay cradled like the pieces of her past, the photographs and postcards of her servant's life. The promises for her future and the future of the prodigal soldier who helped her deliver a forgotten Christmas card.

Laura Briggs

# GHOSTS

## OF

## CHRISTMAS PAST

*An Inspirational Romance from White Rose Publishing*

Pelican Book Group

**Keep Reading for a Special Excerpt** from *Ghosts of Christmas Past*

"Slee-py time, comes to you, on wings of white and blue." The girl sang softly as she rocked the bundle in her arms. Strands of dark hair plastered close to her face above the collar of her hospital robe, a face thin and young beneath its pallor.

"While you sleep, dreams will come, on stars so clear and true..." As she sang, her fingers tucked aside the striped blanket around the sleeping infant's face, revealing tiny flushed cheeks. The slow rocking motion of the nursery chair lulled it closer to her body. The room was silent and dim, except for the winking lights of a Christmas tree in one corner.

The door opened, a nurse on the other side. Beside her was a woman in a business suit carrying a sheaf of papers in a portfolio.

"Miss Libby Taylor?" she said, reading a name affixed to the portfolio. "Are you ready?" She offered her a sympathetic smile.

The girl nodded. "I'm ready," she said. Her mouth pressed inwards as she loosened her hold on the bundle, the woman's arms sliding between her and the child.

"Hello there," crooned the woman, shifting the bundle gently against her shoulder. "Ready to see your new family?" The baby stirred slightly and whimpered.

"There's some papers you'll need to sign, Miss Taylor," the woman continued. "And if you want to talk to them–"

"No," the girl interrupted. "No, I don't. Thanks." Arms now empty, her hands rested on her lap. She watched as the woman turned towards the waiting nurse, carry the baby in her arms. The door closed behind them, two shapes disappearing from behind the square of glass at the top.

The girl closed her eyes. "It's for the best," she whispered. Once, then again, as if to convince herself it was true. Her chair began rocking again, her arms wrapped against her body.

*Slee-py time, comes to you, on wings of white*

*and blue ...*

## Eleven Years Later

The crash of percussion beat a slow tempo from the cordoned-off portion of the club. Chords from a steel guitar throbbed as a woman's voice rose above them.

"Sweet dreams keep haunt-ing me," she sang, "let me be free of all these cares. I don't have time, to lose my mind in the em-brace of what we shared." An aching, tender tone as her hand beat time slowly against her denim-clad thigh.

Her sultry gaze swept the gloomy interior with indifference, beneath a long curtain of black hair coaxed into gentle waves. A short denim jacket over her fitted blouse, tight jeans paired with cowboy boots that had seen more than one season of performances in bars and booze halls.

"Why can't I leave it all behind? The way your touch makes me un-wind..." She slid closer to the microphone, her voice betraying no nervousness or hesitation even as one of the bar's patrons yelled something inappropriate from a table somewhere in the dimness.

Sometimes they threw bottles; those joints kept performers walled off behind a cage of chicken wire, screening them from rowdier patrons. Libby had seen it all in her time, almost twelve years on the road singing country songs in every honky tonk between here and home.

Home. There was a place she hadn't seen in a long, long time. Not that she cared to go back anymore.

*Find the eBook at a Favorite Retailer*

Romance Past, Present…and Future?

That's the question on artist Alice Headley's mind. But she's about to receive a little extra help from three strong-willed figures and the love stories in her past…

# GHOSTS

*of*

Romances Past

Can they help Alice discover the truth about her own romantic past before it's too late?

*An Inspirational Romance from White Rose Publishing*

Pelican Book Group

Visit Laura Briggs's Webpage.

# THE PAPER DOLL

www.paperdollwrites.blogspot.com

for information on
upcoming novels, indie projects,
release dates, and a glimpse
into the process behind the stories...
~ Not to mention the latest giveaways ~

—*And*—

"Like" Author Laura Briggs
on Facebook

http://www.facebook.com/authorlaurabriggs

Printed in Great Britain
by Amazon